P9-BZW-284

The GIFT *of a* LEGACY

OTHER NOVELS BY JIM STOVALL

The Ultimate Gift

The Ultimate Life

The Ultimate Journey

The GIFT of a LEGACY

A NOVEL

JIM STOVALL

THE GIFT OF A LEGACY
Published by David C Cook
4050 Lee Vance View
Colorado Springs, CO 80918 U.S.A.

David C Cook Distribution Canada
55 Woodslee Avenue, Paris, Ontario, Canada N3L 3E5

David C Cook U.K., Kingsway Communications
Eastbourne, East Sussex BN23 6NT, England

The graphic circle C logo is a registered trademark of David C Cook.

LCCN 2013934367
ISBN 978-1-4347-0577-8
eISBN 978-0-7814-1081-6

The Team: Don Pape, John Blase, Nick Lee, Caitlyn Carlson, Tonya Osterhouse, Karen Athen.
Cover Design: Amy Konyndyk
Cover Photo: iStockPhoto

Printed in the United States of America
First Edition 2013

1 2 3 4 5 6 7 8 9 10

032513

ABOUT THE AUTHOR

Jim Stovall is among the most sought-after motivational speakers in the world today. Despite failing eyesight and eventual blindness, he has been a national champion Olympic weightlifter, a successful investment broker, and an entrepreneur. He is the cofounder and president of the Emmy Award–winning Narrative Television Network, which makes movies and television accessible for America's 13 million blind and visually impaired people and their families.

Jim Stovall joined the ranks of Walt Disney, Orson Welles, and four U.S. presidents when he was selected as one of the Ten Outstanding Young Americans. The President's Committee on Equal Employment Opportunity honored him as Entrepreneur of the Year in a ceremony at the U.S. capitol. He has appeared on *Good Morning America* and CNN and has been featured in *Reader's Digest*, *TV Guide*, and *Time* magazine. In June 2000, Jim Stovall joined President Jimmy Carter, Nancy Reagan, and Mother Teresa when he was selected as the International Humanitarian.

He is the author of seventeen books, including the three previous titles in this series, the bestselling *The Ultimate Gift*, *The Ultimate Life*, and *The Ultimate Journey*. *The Ultimate Gift* has been made into a major motion picture by 20th Century Fox. *The Ultimate Life* and *The Ultimate Journey* are in production for films to be released in the future.

Jim Stovall can be reached at 918-627-1000 or via email at Jim@JimStovall.com.

Presented To:

From:

Date:

This book is dedicated to my grandparents, who left me with a legacy of hope and possibilities; my parents, who nurtured the legacy and presented it to me; and all of the great mentors in my life who have left me a legacy to share with others.

OUR LEGACIES

Every footprint that we take
Makes a change where we have passed.
Small things there beneath our heel
Are changing where the print was cast.

What then could any difference make
When ruthless paths our courses take?
Beneath our heel some things will bend
Without the strength to rise again.

Joye Kanelakos

INTRODUCTION

My dear reader, you have paid me the greatest compliment and given me the greatest honor by beginning the trip you and I will take together within these pages. Anytime someone like you is willing to invest their money and, more importantly, their time in one of my books, I feel gratitude and a tremendous sense of responsibility.

This effort represents my seventeenth book. Some of you are old friends who have shared many journeys with me through a number of my books, while others of you are new acquaintances who will be traveling this way for the first time.

My fiction career began with a very special novel entitled *The Ultimate Gift,* which became a major motion picture from 20th Century Fox and starred James Garner, Brian Dennehy, and Abigail Breslin. That story and those characters resonated with so many millions of people around the world—including me—that I kept the characters alive in the sequel, *The Ultimate Life*. That story gave me, and my readers around the world, a deeper connection to Red Stevens, Jason Stevens, Mr. Hamilton, and all the other characters that made the saga come alive. Wanting to travel with those special people one more time, I wrote the novel *The Ultimate Journey*.

Now, knowing that all good things—including stories—must come to an end, we experience *The Gift of a Legacy*. This story, just like the first book, *The Ultimate Gift*, is told from the perspective of Theodore J. Hamilton. Rest assured that Jason Stevens will make his presence felt as he shares the wisdom he received from Red Stevens and passes it on to another in the form of a legacy.

I trust that this story, like the others, will be entertaining, challenging, and enlightening, but more importantly, I hope these characters and this message will travel with you every day of your life and that you will find these messages worthy of being a part of your own life and your own legacy as you live well and leave the best parts of your own wisdom behind to benefit others.

We human beings, in our own frailty, often believe we need to get outside of ourselves, and even outside of our community, in order to travel to a different land to find the things we seek. Only when we look inside can we begin to understand the ultimate gift, which allows us to appreciate everything in the world we have been given, both inside and outside ourselves. Once we find this balance, we can, in the words of Red Stevens, "go home to a place we have never been before."

My wish for you is that all your dreams will come true, and as you stand atop the mountain, having reached each of your goals, you will accept that as an opportunity to dream bigger dreams, set greater goals, and leave a lasting legacy for those who will travel behind you.

Anytime you need to touch base with a fellow traveler, you can reach me at 918-627-1000 or Jim@JimStovall.com. I'm looking forward to your success.

Jim Stovall
2013

CONTENTS

CHAPTER ONE

LIFE AND DEATH

We have life as long as our heart is beating, but we live as long as our heart is filled.

I was remembering the last time Sally May Anderson had graced my office with one of her periodic visits. I just sat at my immense, ornate desk and let my thoughts drift back over the decades, rich with memories of Miss Sally.

When one's life is dedicated to handling people's legal matters, the clients generally limit their visits to times when they're confronted with a crisis or a dilemma of some sort. Miss Sally's appointments were more like an event or a happening that everyone in my law firm anticipated with great eagerness.

My name is Theodore J. Hamilton, Esquire, of Hamilton, Hamilton & Hamilton, Attorneys-at-Law. Of the aforementioned Hamiltons, I am the first. The remaining Hamiltons in our organization are made up of my son and grandson. Having two generations of my progeny competently functioning within our firm gives me a unique perspective. While I am hopefully not over the hill, I certainly have reached the crest from which I can see a long and satisfactory career behind me and, with any luck, some interesting challenges and opportunities ahead of me.

The photos in the montage on my credenza were taken at my eightieth birthday party, which was organized by my colleagues here at the firm. I gazed at each of the photos and noticed that Miss Sally was prominently placed in most of them. Having lived eight decades plus a little gives one an interesting perch from which to observe the world. My half-century of practicing law has brought me satisfying measures of fame and fortune as well as a number of treasured friends. When people are confronted with legal issues, they not only need a competent attorney, they need a caring friend. I like to think of myself as both.

The mementos and trappings of my long career that adorn my office remind me that I am more a product of the twentieth century than of the twenty-first. But if I am a product primarily of the twentieth century, my friend and client Sally May Anderson was clearly a product of and ambassador to the nineteenth century. Miss Sally brought a gentility and wonder for life to everyone and everything around her.

The last time I saw her, she had been rapidly approaching her hundredth birthday. As usual, she wanted to see me about a legal matter pertaining to her home, known by everyone as Anderson House.

Anderson House was originally built in 1862 by Miss Sally's late husband's grandfather, Colonel Milton Anderson. The home was the most spectacular residence of its time and has remained so throughout the ensuing years. When Miss Sally's beloved husband, Leonard, passed away almost fifty years ago, she turned the vintage home into an idyllic bed-and-breakfast. Anderson House

Bed-and-Breakfast became Miss Sally's domain and passion for the next fifty years.

Miss Sally's home was a destination and sanctuary for world travelers, as well as a dining or overnight getaway for city dwellers like me who simply wanted to get out into the country and savor a bygone time in a very special place with some amazing people.

One never knew who might be in residence at Anderson House. During my most recent stay, I met the Heavyweight Champion of the World; a young man named Tracy who was an award-winning filmmaker; a former President of the United States; and a gentleman I will never forget …

Just as I was leaving Anderson House's parlor, which is the gathering place for guests most evenings, I spotted a small, stooped elderly man in a tattered Army uniform. I introduced myself, and he told me his name was Joshua. He had come to Anderson House every year since World War II for a reunion of his regiment. Miss Sally's late husband had been their commander.

Each year, they would come to Anderson House to share old stories and memories, and they would end the reunion by saluting one another.

Joshua lamented, "I'm the last one living, so there's no one here to salute."

I felt a wave of emotion and patriotism and said, "Sir, if you'll accept a heartfelt salute from an old Navy man, I would be honored."

Joshua and I exchanged salutes.

That is just one of my many priceless memories from Anderson House.

Without thinking, I reached forward to the spot on my desk where I knew my cup of tea would be sitting. I had picked up the habit of drinking steaming-hot tea every day sixty years ago during a two-year excursion to Korea, by way of invitation from Uncle Sam. Upon returning to the United States after my stint in the Korean War, I continued to drink tea, but it became a lifelong habit courtesy of a life lesson from Miss Sally May Anderson.

Shortly after passing the bar exam, I opened my law office. At the time, it was not the highly respected firm that Hamilton, Hamilton & Hamilton currently is, housed in our palatial offices. Back then, the shingle outside the door modestly read Hamilton Law Office, and the environment certainly did not give my prospective clients a feeling of confidence.

One particular morning, the bell on the front door of my office rang, hopefully signaling that I had a prospective client, but more likely announcing the arrival of a salesman or another person looking for the dental office down the hall.

I leaped up from my desk and rushed into the outer office, as I was performing all of the receptionist duties in the Hamilton Law Office at that particular point in time. Truth be known, I was handling all of the duties in the office.

I was confronted by the immaculately dressed Sally May Anderson, who stood in the middle of my entryway. She smiled brightly, extended a gloved hand, and proclaimed, "I assume you are Theodore J. Hamilton, Esquire."

I was at a loss for words, so I simply nodded as she continued.

"I am Sally May Anderson, and you have been recommended to me as the right man to handle a unique legal challenge."

I already knew who she was, as she was one of the best-known figures in the region. I couldn't imagine why she was in my office or which of my meager handful of clients had referred her to me.

I motioned her toward my office, and she entered regally, as if she had arrived at the queen's throne room instead of my shabby office. She settled into one of my threadbare hand-me-down client chairs and gazed around the room. She seemed to accept everything at face value without judgment, which was a quality of Miss Sally's I came to respect and tried to emulate throughout the ensuing decades.

I asked if she would like coffee, tea, or anything else to drink, and I was relieved when she declined, as I didn't have anything on the premises to drink other than my tea, which was in a Styrofoam cup in front of me.

I knew from news accounts that Sally May had to be at least twenty years older than me, but that was hard to believe as I looked across my desk at her.

Without preamble, she reached into her purse, took out a porcelain tea cup and saucer, poured my hot tea out of its Styrofoam container into the teacup, and placed the cup back on my desk on the saucer as she tossed the disposable cup into a nearby trash can.

She stated emphatically, "I always carry one with me. Drinking tea is an experience to be savored, not a duty to be performed."

I didn't know what to think or say, so I just nodded as if I understood. She settled back into my client chair, took a deep breath, and began.

"Mr. Hamilton, my late husband left me a fabulous home and considerable resources with which to live the rest of my life. I wish to open my home to others so they can experience the wonders that it offers. I also want to make provisions so that Anderson House can continue to serve others long after I'm gone."

I began taking notes on a legal pad as she continued.

"A young man named Howard Stevens, with whom my late husband had some business dealings, told me you were his attorney and you were the man I needed to see."

Sitting alone in my office fifty years after that initial meeting, I was thankful to my friend Red Stevens for having faith in me and introducing me to Miss Sally.

When one practices law and endeavors to do it well, one deals with every aspect of one's clients' lives. When I started out as a young attorney, most of my clients were young as well. This means that in the early years, I dealt with many legal issues surrounding marriage and childbirth, as well as the launching of careers and businesses. In later decades, an attorney begins dealing with less pleasant legal tasks having to do with death, incapacity, and legacies.

This particular morning started out much as any other. I was the first to arrive at Hamilton, Hamilton & Hamilton, which has been my practice since the beginning, as I like to get my calendar, files, and thoughts organized before the inevitable interruptions from my staff and colleagues encroach.

An hour or so after I arrived, my assistant, Miss Hastings, lightly knocked on my door and entered. That simple knock on the door signaled something of great import and gravity.

Miss Hastings was my first employee when my law practice began to grow. She has remained with me all of these years, for which I am most grateful. To describe her as my right arm would leave out the many proverbial tasks she performs for me that require both my right and left arm, as well as skills and intuition I don't possess.

We have never discussed aloud the exact terms and conditions under which we work, but—over the months, years, and decades—a seamless working relationship and profound friendship has formed. We have never actually discussed that her respectful knock on the door meant anything specific, but we both knew that it did.

Following the knock, she entered solemnly, stood in the middle of my office, and announced in an emotional voice, "Mr. Hamilton, Miss Sally May Anderson passed away in her sleep last night."

CHAPTER TWO

PAST, PRESENT, AND FUTURE

We have a great life when we learn from our past, plan our future, and live each day in the present.

When one loses a special friend, even though that friend is approaching her one-hundredth birthday, it hurts and leaves an empty feeling. Every person who knew Miss Sally and was touched by her understood logically that they couldn't keep a treasured ninety-year-old person in their lives forever. But no amount of logic prepared them for the time when she was gone. Sally Anderson had been a fixture in our community and in my life for so long it was hard to imagine a time or a circumstance when she wouldn't be there.

On the Wall of Fame in my office, there are photos capturing the special times and people in my life and career. As I gazed at the countless photographs that represent the milestones in the life of Theodore Hamilton, it became obvious that a handful of special people had been there with me every step of the way.

Looking at the earliest photo of Sally and me, I was struck with a number of impressions. First, I was amazed that we had ever looked that young. Even though Sally was almost fifty and I was only thirty in the photo, we appeared to be contemporaries in age, but that's where the connection should have ended during that era. Miss Sally and I met and became friends during a time when wealthy, prominent white women like Sally May Anderson didn't do business with, socialize with, or even have their picture taken with a young gentleman of color like me.

Although that reality wasn't printed in any of the law books that I studied or lived my life by, a half-century ago the rules dealing with racial issues may as well have been written in blood.

But Sally seemed to transcend all of that. It wasn't that she was opposed to it or objected in some way. She just seemed to be oblivious to racism and all of the pain it created. She simply rose above it and chose to live her life on a higher plane.

As I looked at that special photo, which captured Sally and me at a place and time that existed a long time ago, I couldn't help but compare it to the last time Sally had been in my office, just a little over a month before.

We never know when our last time in the presence of a dear friend, colleague, mentor, or member of our family will be. I have always believed if you treat each day, each meeting, and each activity as if it were your last, sooner or later you will be right. Each day, the obituaries are filled with names of people who assumed they had decades of life ahead of them. Every day is a gift because it can either be the first day of the rest of our life or be our last day here on earth.

As I have stated, every meeting with Sally was a happening. She never had a routine moment or encounter in her life. Miss Sally treated everyone and everything as if it were special, and somehow it always was.

The days of me flying solo in a one-man office, serving as my own receptionist, secretary, and janitor, are long gone. Today, the firm of Hamilton, Hamilton & Hamilton occupies multiple floors of an upscale high-rise building.

Although very few people in our firm have access to my appointment calendar, somehow everyone in the building seemed to know the day and hour that Sally May Anderson was scheduled to appear. There was more energy in the office, and everyone was infused with a sense of anticipation.

Our security officer, who mans the desk in the lobby on our ground floor, had already phoned to let me know that Miss Sally's car was pulling up to the curb.

One might wonder how a security guard, whose duty requires him to stay seated at his post in the lobby, could tell that one particular car was approaching amidst all the busy downtown rush-hour traffic. But one needed only to get a glimpse of Miss Sally's classic Bentley custom limousine to understand that it's one in a million and could be spotted anywhere.

I made my way to the lobby of our offices, near the elevator, as I wanted to be standing by when Miss Sally emerged.

Our receptionist, Kelly, who is always energetic and engaging, was even more attentive than usual. Kelly is a beautiful young lady with dancing green eyes. She and Miss Sally formed a special kind of connection years ago that none of us ever quite understood.

In anticipation of Miss Sally's visit, Kelly had straightened her desk and put the entire lobby in order. And then, as she always did before one of Miss Sally's visits, Kelly placed an empty flower vase on the corner of her desk.

Several of my partners had found mysterious excuses to be in the lobby near the elevator at that particular moment in time.

As the elevator door slid open, I extended my arm to prevent the door from closing again. First, because at ninety-nine, Miss Sally didn't move as quickly as she used to, and secondly, because elevator rides were never quite long enough for Sally May Anderson, as she always assumed that the brief time huddled with strangers in a confined space was an opportunity to make new friends and introduce everyone. So, as I held the door open, Miss Sally was introducing two people she had just met to one another. Even though these two individuals had worked in this building for many years and had passed one another in the hall or ridden the elevator together countless times, it took Miss Sally to introduce them.

As the door slid closed, I observed the two former strangers chatting amiably, as if they were old friends. All thanks to Miss Sally.

She stepped into the lobby on the arm of her chauffeur, traveling companion, and assistant, Hawthorne. Hawthorne is of indeterminate age, background, and country of origin. All anyone knows and all anyone need know of Hawthorne is that he has been totally devoted and singularly dedicated to Miss Sally May Anderson for almost sixty years.

He would not even contemplate the thought or understand anyone who might suggest that he had reached an age at which he might need his own chauffeur, traveling companion, or assistant. Hawthorne knew that he was put on this earth for the sole task of serving Miss Sally, so he was always ready, willing, and able to do it.

Miss Sally graced me with her smile, which always put me in mind of an eagerly anticipated sunrise. She stepped forward and hugged me warmly, then greeted each of my colleagues who had somehow happened to be in the lobby at that moment.

Then Hawthorne led Miss Sally over to Kelly's reception desk and stepped back, allowing the two ladies a moment to themselves. Miss Sally, knowing that the empty flower vase would be in place for her visit, put some flowers freshly cut from her own garden in the vase on Kelly's desk.

Miss Sally smiled and asked Kelly, "So have you met that special person yet?"

Kelly laughed and replied, "Miss Sally, I'm still working on it and am having fun doing it."

Miss Sally joined in the laughter and stated, "Well, the hunt is often the best part of any relationship, but you really need to find someone better than me to bring you flowers."

Kelly rushed around her desk, hugged Miss Sally, and said, "I don't think there will ever be anybody better than you for that."

Hawthorne stepped forward, and Miss Sally took his arm as we walked into my office.

Miss Sally stood and gazed around my office before she finally nodded as if signifying everything was in its place and all was well.

Only then did she settle into one of the client chairs in front of my desk.

She pointed to the earliest photograph of us, which showed the two of us standing in my very first office. She chuckled and said, "Ted, you found you a really good-lookin' girl to stand next to in that photo."

I smiled and nodded with satisfaction. Miss Sally was one of the few people who ever called me Ted. I was addressed as Sir, Mr. Hamilton, or possibly Theodore, but Miss Sally was comfortable addressing me as Ted, and it made me feel special.

Understanding that legal issues are supposed to be confidential, Hawthorne drifted over to a leather sofa in the corner of my office. He picked up a magazine and pretended to be completely engrossed in whatever was within its pages. I, however, was quite certain that the slightest gesture or nuance from Miss Sally would bring him rushing to her side.

Sally May Anderson had been born and raised with a generation of people who understood and valued small talk. She would never think about coming into someone's office without asking about family members, travel plans, and the condition of their flower garden. After I covered all the pertinent points with her, she reciprocated by sharing about all of the happenings in her life since we had last been together.

Finally, with all of the preliminary matters out of the way, Miss Sally looked directly into my eyes, giving me her full attention, and said, "Theodore, I need to make arrangements for the next phase of my life."

CHAPTER THREE

THE BEQUEST

The successful person leaves behind their values in addition to their valuables and a piece of themselves.

It was hard to know how to respond to a person who had lived almost a century when she told me she needed to make arrangements for the next phase of her life.

A wise old professor in law school once told me, rather emphatically, "Hamilton, the more you listen and the less you talk, the brighter your clients will assume you are."

Trying to keep that admonition in mind, I held my pen poised above a blank legal pad and asked Miss Sally, "How do you see the next phase of your life?"

Sally chuckled and stated in a matter-of-fact fashion, "Well, Ted, the next phase of my life will end with me dying, at which point everything will become your problem. But between now and then, I need to make arrangements for Anderson House and my great-grandson Joey."

Anderson House was and is a totally unique enterprise and piece of real estate. The property comprises hundreds of acres of land and a 150-year-old ornate mansion that could never be replicated or replaced.

For the past fifty years, though running Anderson House was

Miss Sally's joy and passion, it was also an extremely profitable and growing business enterprise.

In addition to Miss Sally's oversight and management and Hawthorne's able assistance in every area of the operation, Anderson House boasts two other lifelong staff members who are totally committed to Anderson House, Miss Sally, and the endless parade of guests who are constantly arriving.

Claudia is a world-renowned chef, baker, and gardener who Miss Sally discovered somewhere in Central Europe. Claudia may be the most versatile chef anywhere in the world. She prepares custom dishes for Anderson House guests that reflect the cuisine of their hometown or country of origin while still allowing them to sample the subtle flavors, tastes, and nuances of the whole world.

Oscar had served as the engineer, carpenter, and handyman at Anderson House when it was the private residence of Miss Sally and her late husband, Leonard Anderson. When the house was converted into the world's greatest bed-and-breakfast, Oscar made sure it kept all of the artistry and craftsmanship of a 150-year-old architectural treasure while offering every modern convenience and state-of-the-art amenity. Maintaining a 150-year-old wood structure with countless passageways, staircases, nooks, and crannies was a labor of love for Oscar. He boasted, "Anderson House and me are both growing old together."

I couldn't imagine Anderson House ever existing without Miss Sally. It wasn't just the best place in the world to visit, dine, or relax; it was a special environment that offered a unique perspective on the world—chiefly because of Miss Sally and her impact on those around her. The thought of anyone taking her place was inconceivable, but the idea of her great-grandson, Joey Anderson, contributing in any way was impossible to imagine.

Joey was somewhere in his mid-twenties. He had always exhibited the unique ability to fail to appreciate, understand, or take advantage of all the treasures in his life while at the same time pursuing every worthless, destructive distraction he could possibly find. Young people like Joey Anderson who are given every possible advantage seem to go out of their way to court misery and failure in spite of everything around them.

Joey had squandered his educational opportunities; rejected everything that his parents, grandparents, and Miss Sally had tried to teach him; and had fled Anderson House and the area as quickly as he was able to do so. Joey had been heli-skiing in Austria, scuba diving around the Great Barrier Reef in Australia, and backpacking across Asia, among every other experience imaginable, but he had never once—to my knowledge—done anything for anyone other than himself. He had spent prodigious amounts of his family's money in the headlong pursuit of his own selfish whims and, despite having everything in the world anyone could ask for, without a single discomfort or responsibility, had managed to become a miserable person with a knack for making everyone around him equally miserable.

I realize that blood is thicker than water, and all people—including Miss Sally—love their children, grandchildren, and great-grandchildren if they're lucky enough to have them. Therefore, regardless of my discomfort in expressing it, I knew that Miss Sally was entitled to and expected my honest and most candid opinion. I took a deep breath and plunged in.

"Miss Sally, Anderson House needs loving care, competent management and oversight, long-term vision with immediate execution, and someone with experience and wisdom. Conversely, what it does not need, by any stretch of the imagination, is any involvement from your great-grandson, Joey Anderson."

Hawthorne picked that moment to vigorously clear his throat, which spoke to his agreement with me as much as if he had offered a standing ovation.

I sat back in my chair, awaiting Miss Sally's argument, anger, or disapproval.

Instead, she just smiled brightly and stated for the record, "Anderson House doesn't need Joey, but Joey needs Anderson House."

As usual, Miss Sally had taken all of my logic, wisdom, and experience, turned it around, and abruptly set it on its ear.

I stuttered, stammered, and started again. "Miss Sally, I'm going to need you to explain that."

She asked, "Ted, do you remember how I came to be your client?"

I nodded and answered, "Red Stevens referred you, didn't he?"

Sally nodded and said, "Red Stevens did many great things in his life for everyone around him, including me. One of the best things he ever did was to introduce me to Theodore J. Hamilton, Attorney-at-Law."

The open wound from the recent loss of my lifelong best friend, Howard "Red" Stevens, was still excruciating, but I tried to focus on the joy his life had brought me and not the pain his death had created.

"Bringing me a client like you at that point in my career was akin to life support," I explained. "But what does Red Stevens's introduction, which happened over fifty years ago, have to do with Anderson House now and in the future?"

"It's quite simple," Miss Sally began to explain. "I learned about all the lessons that Red Stevens taught his grandson, Jason Stevens, through the portion of his will that has become known as the Ultimate Gift."

What had started out as a private bequest known only to Red Stevens and me, which I had crafted into a legal document under Red's direction, became a worldwide media event after Red Stevens's death.

Howard "Red" Stevens had amassed a multi-billion-dollar fortune derived from his holdings in oil, cattle, and a vast number of diversified business holdings. He'd called me shortly after I completed law school with only two things on his mind. I can still hear his voice echoing across the decades.

"I've got a world to conquer, and I need a lawyer."

I was trying to think of a tactful way to inform him over the phone that I was an African-American, and he might prefer to look elsewhere. But like Miss Sally, Red Stevens was color-blind. He interrupted my faltering attempt to apprise him of the situation and asked, "You are Theodore J. Hamilton, and you did graduate first in your class, did you not?"

I blurted, "Yes, sir," and Red's only response to that situation—and every challenge over the next fifty years—was his emphatic declaration, "Well, then, let's get started."

Late in his life, my friend realized that he had succeeded in business but was in jeopardy of failing at life. I remember him lamenting, "Ted, what's the use of having everything and learning everything over a lifetime if you can't share it with the people you love?"

From that point, Red Stevens focused all of his considerable energy on the challenge of overcoming a lifelong period of neglect as he organized a crash course in everything that matters for his grandson, Jason Stevens.

When I think of Jason Stevens before his grandfather's death, he puts me very much in mind of Joey Anderson. After his grandfather's death, Jason showed up late for Red's funeral with a bad attitude and a chip on his shoulder. He nearly missed the family meeting where I read the will to the heirs. Jason simply excused his tardiness and bad attitude by saying, "I know what he left me … nothing."

Red had instructed me to craft a unique document as a codicil to his will. It provided for Jason to undertake an odyssey for a year, during which time he would experience twelve gifts, or life lessons, designed by his grandfather. The will stated that if Jason could satisfactorily navigate each of the tasks set before him, he would then receive his inheritance, mysteriously known only as "The Ultimate Gift."

The transformation that the Ultimate Gift experience wrought in Jason Stevens was nothing short of miraculous. Jason became a responsible, productive, generous young man with $2 billion of his grandfather's money that he was using to literally change the world around him.

I certainly understood Miss Sally's desire to have an influence on her great-grandson like Red Stevens had provided for Jason, but I had to point out to her, "Miss Sally, I agree that Joey could certainly benefit from a strong dose of Red Stevens's Ultimate Gift, but as you know, regrettably, Red Stevens isn't here with us any more."

Sally sat up straight, smiled with anticipation, and stated emphatically, "I'm well aware of the fact that Red isn't here any more, but Jason is!"

CHAPTER FOUR

THE MEETING

Every great legacy starts with a great life, and every great life starts with a great plan.

A heavy fog hung over Anderson House and the surrounding grounds like a shroud. I had been on the property for several hours, having actually enjoyed my first cup of coffee on the upper veranda as I observed the sunrise trying to cut through the dense haze. I am a confirmed lifelong tea drinker, but I just can't seem to get a day started off right without my morning coffee.

Morning is always the best part of the day, at least from my point of view, at Anderson House. I wondered if it would still remain as special in the future without Sally May Anderson there to brighten each daybreak.

I have participated in private meetings in the Oval Office, argued weighty matters before the Supreme Court, and conducted board meetings with millionaires, billionaires, superstars, and the like, but the most challenging, stimulating, inspiring, and thought-provoking discussions of my life have taken place around the breakfast table at Anderson House. There are a few special places on earth where the best, brightest, and most significant examples of humanity tend to gather. Great institutions of higher learning, places of worship, and seats of government are examples of these locations.

If you ask anyone who has ever spent any time at Anderson House, they will invariably inform you that Miss Sally's breakfast table rivaled anywhere in the world as a gathering place for the best, brightest, and most formidable among us.

Preparations for Sally May Anderson's memorial service had been under way for several days, and it would be conducted on the grounds of Anderson House. As the executor of Miss Sally's estate, it was my responsibility to be on hand. As her friend, it was my privilege to make sure everything was as it should be.

Over the previous seventy-two hours, we had received notices and requests from heads of state, titans of industry, entertainment elite, and representatives from the royal family that they wanted to make arrangements to be on hand to pay their respects.

I pulled my small leather-bound notebook from the inner-breast pocket of my best suit, flipped it open, and reviewed all of the arrangements and each of the copious notes I had taken to ensure all would be in readiness.

Claudia stepped onto the veranda and unobtrusively refilled my coffee cup, being careful not to disturb me. I closed my notebook and placed it back in my jacket pocket.

"Thank you, Claudia." I nodded at my steaming cup of coffee and continued with a sigh. "Well, it's going to be a hard but special day. I just hope I've taken care of everything."

Without hesitating, Claudia responded, "Mr. Hamilton, it seems that no stone has been left unturned, and everyone has done their utmost for Miss Sally, but you remember what she always said."

I did, indeed, remember, and it caused me to chuckle as I emphatically stated in unison with Claudia, "All you can do is all you can do."

That phrase, and the sentiment behind it, was one of my lasting legacies from Miss Sally. With that simple phrase, Sally May Anderson had encouraged a myriad of people countless times. When you heard Miss Sally utter, "All you can do is all you can do," you felt duty-bound to give your best effort and confident knowing it would be good enough.

My cell phone vibrated, and I glanced down to see that Hawthorne was calling. I answered promptly, and he greeted me respectfully and began reporting on the litany of details to which he had already attended that morning. Hawthorne, Claudia, and Oscar had done yeoman's work over the past few days, getting everything in and around Anderson House ready. Hawthorne concluded the call with the question that always seemed to be on his lips after he had completed another job to his accustomed high standard.

"Will there be anything else, sir?"

I told him I couldn't think of anything, thanked him, and closed my phone.

Taking one last sip of the gourmet coffee Claudia had just poured and taking one last gaze across the gardens below, I turned to go downstairs and prepare myself to do what needed to be done.

The swelling strains of Pachelbel's Canon drifted out from the full orchestra that was playing beside the dais that had been set up on the grounds of Anderson House for Miss Sally's memorial service. I stood beside the walkway along which mourners drifted uphill to the seating area.

While the faces and identities of most of those attending the service would have been immediately recognizable to anyone who regularly reads a newspaper or watches television, my stalwart assistant and right arm, Miss Hastings, was by my side to fill in the blanks by whispering in my ear the names of virtually every person as they approached us.

I was pleased to see my old friend Gus Caldwell striding up the hill between a United States senator and a business mogul. Red Stevens had introduced me to Gus years ago. The two of them had built oil, cattle, and business empires that may never be duplicated again.

Gus hugged Miss Hastings and greeted her warmly and then extended his hand to shake mine. Gus Caldwell is a man of the outdoors. I knew he would have been more comfortable astride his horse than he was now, elegantly dressed in the somber suit befitting the occasion. As he shook my hand vigorously, I had the same fleeting thought I always had when shaking hands with Gus: He could break my hand without even trying.

Gus said, "Ted, it's good to see you, my friend." He released my hand, no worse for wear, and continued, "She was a special lady. They don't make 'em like Miss Sally anymore, and I will always be grateful to Red for introducing me to her."

Just then, Jason Stevens stepped out of the stream of people walking up the hill and approached us. He greeted us all warmly and respectfully. I couldn't help but remember when I had first met him, which had happened during a time in his life when he didn't show a bit of respect for anyone or anything.

If anyone but Red Stevens had asked me to shepherd young Jason Stevens through the twelve life lessons that his grandfather had prepared for him, I wouldn't have even considered it.

Gus grinned at Jason and said playfully, "After this service, you and I will need to walk around the perimeter of the grounds and make sure all of Miss Sally's fences are shipshape."

Jason's eyes grew wide for an instant, and then he realized Gus was observing that time-honored cowboy tradition of pulling his leg.

The first of Red Stevens's gifts to Jason had come in the form of lessons about work, delivered by Gus Caldwell, who remained an unparalleled example of the merits of hard work. Jason had spent a month straining his back to build a fence while he also strained his mind to learn about the gift of work.

As the last few guests took their places, Gus, Jason, Miss Hastings, and I walked down the aisle and found our seats in the front row.

Funeral services are a difficult proposition. While you want to pay attention to everyone present and every word said, each person and every thought uttered takes you to past places and times in your own life during which the honored person touched you. I found myself being absorbed by memories and fond thoughts of Miss Sally as the memorial service played out.

I heard the orchestra playing the refrains of one of Miss Sally's favorite pieces and knew that it was approaching the time in the service when I was to speak. As the symphony's last notes drifted across the grounds of Anderson House, I approached the podium.

"For anyone who knew Miss Sally in life, there is nothing I need say at this point to immortalize her in your mind, heart, and spirit. And for any unfortunate soul who never met Sally May Anderson, there's nothing I can say to describe the special person and significant life we celebrate today."

I reached into my pocket, took out a single piece of paper, unfolded it, and set it on the podium before me. As I glanced down at the impactful words, I realized I wouldn't need the paper, as the words on the paper had been seared into my brain and etched into my heart years before.

"Miss Sally had a favorite poem that was given to her by the same person who gave it to me—my lifelong friend, Red Stevens. Today is the day Miss Sally determined we should give it to you."

I looked out over the expectant crowd. Just as I was preparing to speak, the sun broke through the fog, causing the gardens and grounds of Anderson House to come to life and display their vivid colors. I nodded and smiled, knowing that some things are just meant to be. And then I began to recite …

"CORNERSTONES

"If I am to dream, let me dream magnificently.
Let me dream grand and lofty thoughts and ideals
That are worthy of me and my best efforts.

"If I am to strive, let me strive mightily.
Let me spend myself and my very being
In a quest for that magnificent dream.

"And, if I am to stumble, let me
stumble but persevere.
Let me learn, grow, and expand myself
to join the battle renewed—
Another day and another day and another day.

"If I am to win, as I must, let me do so
with honor, humility, and gratitude
For those people and things that
have made winning possible
And so very sweet.

"For each of us has been given life
as an empty plot of ground
With four cornerstones.
These four cornerstones are the ability to dream,
The ability to strive,
The ability to stumble but persevere,
And the ability to win.

"The common man sees his plot
of ground as little more

Than a place to sit and ponder the
things that will never be.
But the uncommon man sees his
plot of ground as a castle,
A cathedral,
A place of learning and healing.
For the uncommon man understands
that in these four cornerstones
The Almighty has given us
anything—and everything."

I paused briefly to allow the words of that poem to sink in for all of us gathered there to honor Miss Sally.

Just as I was preparing to give my final remarks, I heard the roar of a speeding motorcycle thundering up the hill.

CHAPTER FIVE

THE INHERITANCE

If I could help someone like me, it would be my legacy.

Up to that point, it had been what my sainted mother would have called a banner day. Miss Sally's memorial service was shaping up to be all that I hoped it would be and more. The best, brightest, and most-celebrated people of Sally's generation and several subsequent generations had gathered to pay respects to her and pay tribute to a life well lived.

The orchestra had performed flawlessly. Each of the speakers had been thoughtful and poignant, and the weather had even cooperated when, as if on cue, the fog parted and the sun broke through, almost as though Miss Sally were sending us her love from heaven. I felt good about what I had shared and had gotten through the reading of the special poem without stumbling.

And then, just when I thought everything was under control, some imbecilic half-wit on a motorcycle raced through the parking area below and actually began riding the motorcycle up the walkway toward the area where everyone was seated for the memorial service. The infernal contraption was so loud I couldn't even think, much less conclude my remarks to those assembled for the solemn occasion.

I have spent over a half century of my life in the practice of the law. In most legal circles, I am considered formidable, and in others, I am actually thought of as intimidating. As I stood at the podium, looking over the impressive group of people that had gathered for the memorial service, I was contemplating what civil, criminal, and punitive legal action could be taken against the incorrigible individual who dared to interrupt Miss Sally May Anderson's tribute. I was mentally reviewing all of the pro and con arguments surrounding the death penalty as everyone turned in unison to stare at the huge motorcycle that was thundering toward them.

As it approached the back row of seated people, I hoped the lunatic driving the motorcycle would come to a stop before plowing into several rows of chairs. At the very last moment, he did indeed slow the vehicle and turn it parallel to the back row before he finally brought it to a halt.

As the motorcycle's deafening engine mercifully shut off, the silence that fell over the hillside was a welcome relief.

As the rider got off of the motorcycle and casually tossed his helmet aside as if he would never need it again, he brushed back long, stringy hair, and I instantly recognized him from some of Miss Sally's photos. It was Joey Anderson. Eventually, the crowd settled down and turned toward where I was still standing at the podium. I tried to think of what to say and how to get everyone's mind and spirit back on Miss Sally, the life she lived, and what she would want us to take away from this day. I cleared my throat and resumed speaking.

"Miss Sally May Anderson lived an incredible life. One need look no further than the luminaries gathered here out of respect for her to understand the impact her life had on past and current generations."

I paused and then stared directly at Joey as I concluded my remarks.

"Miss Sally would want us to learn from her past and celebrate her memory in the present, but most of all, she would want us to look to the future as her love, energy, and wisdom still need to be experienced by certain individuals."

I glared at Joey and finished by saying, "May we all dedicate ourselves to the task of ensuring that the lessons Miss Sally left behind be felt by those who need them most."

The memorial service concluded without further incident. I stood with Miss Hastings, Gus, and Jason to thank everyone as they filed back down the footpath toward the sumptuous feast Claudia had set out on linen-covered tables in the garden area.

As the last of the mourners passed by and I thanked them for being a part of the special day, Jason glanced over toward where Joey was nonchalantly making some type of adjustment to his motorcycle. He was self-absorbed and seemed completely oblivious to what was going on around him and the fact that he had disrespectfully interrupted a solemn occasion.

Jason said aloud to no one in particular, "He sort of reminds me of me, but I couldn't have been that bad."

Miss Hastings began trying to assure Jason that he hadn't been that difficult or a problem, when Gus Caldwell blurted out in his matter-of-fact tone, "Son, you weren't that bad … You were a whole lot worse."

I wasn't able to enjoy as much of Claudia's culinary artistry as I would have liked. I floated from table to table, trying to make everyone feel welcome as I knew Miss Sally would have done if she had been there. I checked on a number of details regarding the food and beverage service only to find that everything had already been handled by Claudia and double-checked by Hawthorne.

The day had turned out to be bright and warm, and the gardens were idyllic, so the guests lingered, sharing their stories and memories of Miss Sally and how she had touched each of their lives.

Eventually, the guests began to drift away amidst hugs, handshakes, and well wishes. Finally, there were only a few of us left to tend to the cleanup.

Joey Anderson drifted over toward me and mumbled, "Are you Hamilton?"

I turned to him with my best courtroom stare and declared, "Young man, I am Theodore J. Hamilton, Esquire."

Joey took a half step back and stared at me as if he were looking at a space alien.

After a long, awkward pause, he explained, "I'm Joey. I was diving near the Great Barrier Reef in Australia when I got your express package about my great-grandmother dying."

He stared at me hopefully, as if I would pick up on his intentions, but I just stared at him, refusing to make it any easier.

He dropped his gaze, cleared his throat, and continued.

"I came here to get my money."

I smiled mischievously and asked, "Did you have some money here?"

He shook his head and whined, "Your letter said I should come and get my stuff."

I feigned confusion and declared, "My correspondence indicated, as I remember, that your great-grandmother, Miss Sally May Anderson, had regrettably passed away, and you should travel by the most expedient conveyance to participate in her memorial service and discuss your possible inclusion in the disposition of her estate."

I took that opportunity to glare disgustedly toward the motorcycle and remark, "I look forward to the point in time when you and I will be able to have a frank and candid discussion regarding the definition of an expedient conveyance."

His confusion turned into annoyance, and he shot back, "Just tell me how I can get my money and get out of here."

I explained, "Young man, there is a time and place for everything, and the time for that discussion will be tomorrow morning, and the place will be around the breakfast table in the main house."

I turned and departed, leaving him standing there, stunned and bewildered.

After enjoying a comfortable evening as a guest of Anderson House, the next morning—as I had done hundreds of times over the years—I made my way toward what I would always think of as Miss Sally's breakfast table.

Anderson House is a rambling old estate with many twists and turns. Guests have been known to get lost, confused, or totally turned around; but every morning, one need simply follow their nose toward the sumptuous aroma emanating from Claudia's kitchen to find their place at Miss Sally's famous breakfast table.

As I settled into my comfortable seat at the head of the table, I couldn't help but think about all of the world leaders, sports and entertainment luminaries, theologians, and thought leaders, as well as everyday people like me who had gathered around this table to take in a bit of sustenance for their body and a lot of sustenance for their mind and spirit.

Generally, all the guests of Anderson House are welcome at this table; however, arrangements for this particular morning had already been planned by Miss Sally on her visit to my office several months before. All the other guests of Anderson House would be breakfasting on the upper veranda or in the main dining room so that a select few of Miss Sally's choosing could have a special meeting over breakfast at this particular table.

Just as Claudia presented me with that cup of pure ambrosia known as the first coffee of the day, Gus Caldwell slid into the seat beside me. I mentally patted myself on the back for beating Gus to the breakfast table, as he has always been known as an early riser.

My private celebration was interrupted when Gus proclaimed, "Beautiful morning, Ted. I've already hiked around the lake on the far end of the property and checked out a few of the outbuildings."

Miss Hastings took her place at my other side. As she and I exchanged our subtle nods to one another that said nothing and expressed everything, Jason Stevens bounded into the room and slid into the chair next to her.

Only after Jason had settled did Hawthorne and Oscar approach the table and look to me for a nod to be seated. Claudia stood expectantly near the door to the kitchen. I smiled and motioned to her, signaling she should serve everyone and join us.

The chair at the opposite end of the table was conspicuously empty.

As their duties always called them elsewhere, Claudia, Hawthorne, and Oscar were not in the habit of joining guests for Miss Sally's famous breakfast gatherings, but today they were able to join in on the stories and remembrances of Miss Sally. We laughed, cried, and shared memories of the special lady and how she had left her imprint on us all.

The breakfast banquet contained every imaginable variety of fresh fruit, pastries, eggs, and all of the other dishes one would expect as well as some one wouldn't. Second cups of coffee were savored, and third cups were enjoyed by a few of us.

Finally, I heard my long-awaited guest of honor and new client approaching. Joey Anderson rounded the corner and stood in the entryway to the breakfast room. The conversation around the table ceased, and the room fell silent as everyone stared at Joey. His hair was a mess, his eyes were red-rimmed, and his clothes looked as if he had slept in them.

Gus broke the silence, speaking to me. "Ted, I think you may have had one of those senior moments they talk about. You must have told Joey we were meeting for lunch instead of breakfast."

Amid the laughter, Joey slunk over to the table and slumped into the chair at the far end.

Claudia asked him what he would like, and Joey just shook his head, grumbling, "I don't eat breakfast."

Gus responded to Joey, "Well, son, if I got out of bed when you did, I wouldn't eat breakfast either."

Joey finally found his voice and a modicum of courage, declaring to everyone, "Look, I don't know you people, and I really don't want to. I just want to know how quick I can get my money and get as far away from this place as possible."

I took Joey's cue and reached into a briefcase near the base of my chair. I set a two-hundred-page document on the corner of the table and smiled at Joey.

"Joey, it's not quite that simple."

He just stared at me, dumbfounded, so I explained, "Your great-grandmother came to me several months ago and asked me to replicate some tenets of the last will and testament of our mutual friend Howard 'Red' Stevens. Those particular provisions of Red Stevens's will dealt with Jason Stevens."

I motioned toward Jason. Joey and Jason nodded at each other perfunctorily.

I continued, "The details will all become clear to you in time, but for the purposes of this meeting, suffice it to say that you have not inherited any money or other assets."

Joey blurted out something unintelligible.

I held my palm out toward him to silence him and continued. "However, you may figure in the future ownership of Anderson House if and only if you are willing to take up residence here and accept the bequest Red Stevens left to Jason as a provision of your great-grandmother's will."

Joey sat in stunned bewilderment.

I glanced at Miss Hastings and asked, "Anything else?"

She rose and gathered up the papers I had set out on the table as she spoke.

"No, sir, that about covers it for this morning. We will continue this discussion tomorrow morning if Joey decides to stay on."

Miss Hastings smiled at Gus Caldwell and asked sweetly, "Gus, since Joey is not familiar with the schedule here at Anderson House, I'm wondering if you could drop around his room tomorrow before breakfast and help him get to the right place at the right time."

Gus nodded and said, "Yes, ma'am. I'll take care of it. I believe I've got my cattle prod out in the truck."

Jason laughed nervously, stating, "I will be here early for breakfast."

Jason had experienced Gus's cattle prod as an abrupt substitute for an alarm clock during the month he was learning about the gift of work.

I rose and said, "My thanks to all. Same time, same place tomorrow."

CHAPTER SIX

THE LEGACY OF WORK

Our work is how we give ourselves to the world and leave a legacy behind.

Joey jumped up from his chair so abruptly it fell over backward and crashed to the floor. He ran from the room and could be heard stomping up the stairs just before the sound of the slamming door to his room reverberated throughout the house.

Everyone around the breakfast table looked at me expectantly. I was trying to formulate some kind of excuse, explanation, or statement to cover Joey Anderson's behavior when my thoughts were interrupted by an infernal commotion involving screeching guitars and pounding drums. Everyone automatically gazed at the ceiling in the direction from which the sound was emanating. It could be felt as much as heard.

I raised my voice so everyone could hear my question. "What in the world is that?"

Sometimes facts, knowledge, and information come from the most unlikely places. Hawthorne cleared his throat, looked at me, and responded, "Mr. Hamilton, sir, I believe that is Maximilian Swayne and his band.... It's from their latest album, if I'm not mistaken."

Knowing that Hawthorne was more a product of my generation than of Joey's, I blurted, "How do you know that?"

"Well, sir," Hawthorne explained, "he was a dear friend of Miss Sally's, and he and the band actually worked on some of their latest compositions here at Anderson House."

I was bewildered and confused, but I nodded at Hawthorne as if that were the most logical explanation I had ever heard.

I thanked everyone and headed up the stairs to confront my latest client and the heir to Sally May Anderson's unique bequest. I didn't knock on Joey's door, as I was certain he wouldn't be able to hear it anyway.

When I peeked inside, I saw Joey stretched across the bed as the cacophony continued from the stereo speakers in his room. Eventually, he glanced in my direction and gave me a look somewhere between annoyance and disgust. I motioned for him to turn down the music, and he hesitated but finally complied.

He addressed me rather loudly, as someone naturally does when they've been listening to music that loudly—or standing behind a jet engine. "I don't like people telling me what music to listen to or how loud I should listen to it."

I smiled amicably and said, "I totally agree. I believe that's Maximilian Swayne and his band. From their latest album, if I'm not mistaken."

Joey looked at me as if I had sprouted wings or grown an extra head.

I continued, "I can honestly say every time I listen to Maximilian Swayne's music, it is at least that loud."

Somehow, thanks to a musician I had not even been aware of ten minutes earlier, Joey and I—at least for the moment—had found some common ground.

Joey sat on the edge of his bed, and I took a seat in a wingback chair facing him.

Patience is a tool, or sometimes a weapon, that comes to those of us who have enjoyed over eighty years here on earth. I just stared at Joey contentedly, prepared to wait all day, until he finally spoke.

"I think you ought to at least tell me what's going on."

I nodded amiably and responded, "I totally agree."

I waited until he asked, "So what do I have to do to get my money?"

"Son," I explained, "if you already have some money, you don't have to do anything to get it, but you're not going to get any more here. At least not in the near term."

Joey slammed his hand down on the bed and blurted, "This whole thing is bogus. I knew I shouldn't have come here."

I smiled, ignored his outburst, and continued. "But your great-grandmother did—as I stated earlier—make provisions for you in her will."

"What's the deal?" he asked.

I smiled and declared, "I'm glad you asked. Her will, as it relates to you, provides for you to receive your inheritance only if you will take up uninterrupted residence here at Anderson House and are willing to learn the lessons your great-grandmother set forth that mirror the Ultimate Gift provisions of Red Stevens's will.

"Red's grandson, Jason, has generously agreed to guide you on this journey. Any time you wish to leave, you are free to go, but only if you complete each of the lessons will you be made aware of your inheritance and receive it."

Joey ranted and complained bitterly, utilizing some language I promised my sainted mother I would not utilize or repeat.

Suffice it to say, despite all of Joey's complaints and protestations, he and Gus Caldwell came down the stairs the next morning at the appointed hour to take their places at the breakfast table. Jason Stevens and Miss Hastings were already there, and Hawthorne and Oscar joined us as Claudia, once again, served a sumptuous breakfast.

I thanked everyone for being a part of the work-in-progress that Miss Sally had asked me to handle. I nodded toward Joey so there would be no mistaking the object of my comments.

He blurted, "I don't understand—"

Gus piped up, "Well, we agree on that, but at least I was able to get you out of bed this morning without the cattle prod."

Jason laughed uncomfortably. The mention of the cattle prod obviously invoked some unpleasant memories for him.

I continued, "Joey, the first lesson is work, and your guide for this entire experience will be Jason."

I nodded to Jason, and he began, "Joey, I have been exactly where you are. I was born wealthy and had everything I thought I wanted but absolutely nothing that I needed to live a fulfilling life. Trust-fund babies like you and me automatically think of work as something someone else does for us. My first lesson in work began with a message from my grandfather that I want to share with you."

Jason punched a button on a remote control he'd set on the table beside him. The large flat-screen television across the room came to life, and I once again saw the image of my best friend. He was never far from my thoughts, but seeing him larger than life on the screen in front of me released a flood of memories and emotions.

He began to speak.

"Jason, when I was much younger than you are now, I learned the satisfaction that comes from a simple four-letter word: work. One of the things my wealth has robbed from you and the entire family is the privilege and satisfaction that comes from doing an honest day's work.

"Now, before you go off the deep end and reject everything I'm going to tell you, I want you to realize that work has brought me everything I have and everything that you have. I regret that I have taken from you the joy of knowing that what you have is what you've earned.

"My earliest memories in the swamps of Louisiana are of work—hard, backbreaking labor that as a young man I resented greatly. My parents had too many mouths to feed and not enough food, so if we wanted to eat, we worked. Later, when I was on my own and came to Texas, I realized that hard work had become a habit for me, and it has served as a true joy all the rest of my life.

"Jason, you have enjoyed the best things that this world has to offer. You have been everywhere, seen everything, and done everything. What you don't understand is how much pleasure these things can bring you when you have earned them yourself, when leisure becomes a reward for hard work instead of a way to avoid work."

The image of my friend faded away as if it were some sort of mist that could not be held or grasped.

Jason addressed Joey and the rest of the group.

"As we go through each of the lessons my grandfather and your great-grandmother planned for us, we will have some special people who are frequent guests of Anderson House assisting us. But when it comes to the gift of work, there's no one better to learn from than my friend Gus Caldwell over there."

Gus nodded at Jason and smiled at Joey, stating, "Jason, I'll be glad to serve."

I knew the process had started, and I hoped Joey would succeed with his bequest as Jason had with Red Stevens's Ultimate Gift legacy.

I retired to my room and packed my bags, preparing to leave Anderson House and trusting the lesson of work to Jason and Gus Caldwell.

But I couldn't leave without walking up the small knoll that was the highest spot on the Anderson House grounds. Near the summit, Miss Sally had been laid to rest next to her husband,

Leonard. As I approached the two headstones—one that had weathered a half century in that spot and the other that had only been in place for a day—I noticed another mourner next to Miss Sally's grave.

Cooper is a beautiful tan canine of indeterminate origin. He had been Miss Sally's constant companion for the past ten years of her life. I had often made fun of Miss Sally for talking to the dog, but over the ensuing years, I had found conversing with Cooper to be quite satisfying and stimulating. He never questioned, complained, or argued. He simply stared at me with eyes that had a depth of understanding and acceptance that I have rarely found among humans.

I looked at him and said, "I miss her too, and I wish I could stay here on this spot from now on, but we've got to be about our business and do what Miss Sally would expect us to do."

Cooper tilted his head and sighed a bit. I spent another minute with Miss Sally and then turned to leave. Cooper walked beside me as we moved away from the fresh grave. He stopped a short distance away and turned to look at the grave again.

I tried to reassure him.

"Don't worry, boy. We can come back any time we want."

As we headed back down the hill toward the immense, stately house, I saw Gus Caldwell's pickup truck bounding up the hill with Joey in the passenger seat. Gus waved and stopped the truck beside Cooper and me.

He rolled down his window and called, "Hello."

I waved at them as I approached the driver's-side window and noticed Joey staring off into the distance distractedly.

I shook hands with Gus and said, "I just wanted to say goodbye to Miss Sally before I headed back into town for a few days."

Gus looked down at Cooper and chuckled, declaring, "Well, it looks like you got a good sidekick there." He pointed his thumb toward Joey and continued, "That's a whole lot more than I can say."

I looked past Gus at Joey and said, "Yeah, I can see you've got your work cut out for you."

Gus announced, "I was looking over the lay of the land earlier, and I determined that Miss Sally and Leonard should have gardens with paths and benches all around their gravesites. There should be a stone walkway up to the top of the knoll, and the whole thing should be surrounded by a sturdy wrought-iron fence."

Gus and I laughed as he continued his drive up the hill. I watched the truck fading into the distance and remembered the fence that Jason had built on Gus's ranch. And I remembered Gus telling me that not only do good fences make good neighbors, but good workers make good fences.

CHAPTER SEVEN

THE LEGACY OF MONEY

We will leave many legacies behind. Money is an important tool but the least valuable of all our legacies.

My trip back to the city and my office was uneventful.

Anderson House is just a few hours and a million light years away from the hustle and bustle of the metropolitan area where I live and work. I slipped back into my normal routine handling court dates and other legal matters, but my thoughts were never far from Miss Sally, Anderson House, and the challenges and opportunities that faced Joey.

Gus Caldwell was never one for a lot of detailed communication. He was fond of saying, "If I need a hand, I'll give you a call. Otherwise, just count on everything getting done." Hawthorne, however, took it upon himself to keep me posted on the daily activities of Gus, Jason, and Joey, as well as their progress on the renovations surrounding Miss Sally's gravesite.

I was ensconced in my office, engrossed in a complex corporate contract, when Miss Hastings tapped on my door and entered. She allowed me to finish reading the clause I was focused on, and then, when I looked up, she announced, "Mr. Hamilton, I just heard from Anderson House, and they're ready for the next meeting tomorrow morning."

Never wanting to miss an opportunity to experience that magnificent place, I finished up the contract, and Miss Hastings joined me for the drive to Anderson House that afternoon.

Hawthorne greeted us at the front steps and whisked our luggage to our adjoining rooms. Claudia greeted us with tea and refreshments while Oscar filled me in on all the details regarding the work that had been done atop the knoll where Leonard and Miss Sally had been laid to rest.

I went upstairs to unpack and to settle into my familiar room. I rested a bit, as people in their eighties should do from time to time, then donned clothes more fitting for Anderson House's pastoral setting and headed across the property toward the knoll.

The first improvement I noticed was the wonderful native-rock walkway that meandered up the hill with shrubs, plants, and flower beds strategically located on either side. As I walked along the walkway, I tried to imagine the amount of work that had been done to gather, move, and set each rock in the interlocking pattern.

As I reached the top of the knoll, a gate set in a six-foot-high wrought-iron fence that stretched into the distance confronted me. There was an arch above the gate with an inscription that read, "In memory of Leonard and Sally Anderson." I opened the gate and wandered through the idyllic network of paths, gardens, and benches that surrounded the gravesite.

In the far corner of the enclosure, I heard voices, so I headed in that direction.

I was greeted by Gus's booming voice shouting, "Hello!"

As I got closer, I could see Jason waving at me energetically and wearing a smile that stretched from ear to ear.

He called, "Mr. Hamilton, have you ever seen anything more perfect than this?"

I shook my head and responded, "No, Jason. I can't imagine anything better for Miss Sally and Leonard."

I looked at Joey, who was leaning against a shovel. He was covered with dirt and sweat and seemed about ready to collapse.

I said, "Hello, Joey."

He waved halfheartedly and muttered, "Hi."

I observed the surroundings again and stated, "Well, you must be really proud of what's been done here."

Joey replied, "Yeah, it's pretty nice, but I don't see why we couldn't get somebody to do all this work."

Gus roared with laughter, slapped Joey on the back—nearly knocking him to the ground—and declared, "Son, we did get somebody to do all this work … You."

Jason explained, "Joey, I know it doesn't feel like it right now, but you will come back to this spot many times throughout your life to pay your respects to your great-grandparents. You will never be able to look at that fence or these gardens without feeling good about yourself."

As Gus, Jason, and Joey loaded the remaining tools and supplies into Gus's truck, I walked over to spend a few moments with Miss Sally. I looked all around the idyllic gardens that provided a fitting final resting place for my special friend and said to her,

"Well, old girl, he did it. I just hope the rest of the lessons take root like this one did."

As the sun melted from the western horizon and twilight gathered, I closed the wrought-iron gate and headed back toward Anderson House.

The next morning, my first cup of coffee and I were on the veranda to welcome the first hint of sunrise. Gus stepped out to say good-bye and let me know he was heading back to his ranch in Texas. I hugged the bear of a man, who seemed more like the granite statue of a rugged pioneer than an old man who was at least my age.

I said, "Gus, I don't know how to thank you."

"Ted," he explained, "I'm not going to tell you how much trouble you would have been in if you hadn't called on me for this little project. Red and I discovered years ago that if you build a fence, it can go all the way around your property, but if you build a fence-builder, the fence can go all the way around the world."

Miss Hastings and Jason, along with two other guests of Anderson House, were already at the breakfast table when I arrived.

The first new guest was recognizable to anyone who has ever followed finance or presidential politics. I smiled, extended my hand, and declared, "Mr. Forbes, it's great to see you again."

He shook my hand warmly and responded, "Ted, it's always good to see you. We have solved many of the world's problems sitting around this very table, and I understand we have another little challenge to take care of today."

I nodded affirmatively and turned to the other gentleman. While Steve Forbes looked like he had just stepped out of a meeting in a Wall Street boardroom, the individual standing next to him, with his long, curly hair and an unruly beard, put me in mind of sketches I have seen of the artist Leonardo DaVinci.

Hawthorne did the honors and intoned, "Mr. Theodore Hamilton, this is Maximilian Swayne, a treasured friend of Miss Sally's and longtime frequent guest of Anderson House."

I shook hands with the musician and said, "It's a pleasure to meet you. I have only recently become aware of your work."

He laughed and said, "I'm surprised you've heard of me at all."

I feigned shock and announced, "I'll have you know I was just listening to your latest album the other day right here in this very house."

Just as everyone was being seated and Claudia was serving our breakfast, Joey shuffled in groggily and slumped into the chair at the opposite end of the table. I could see the blisters on his hands from my end of the long table, and he moved as if every joint and muscle in his body ached.

He glanced up as Claudia set a plate before him and noticed Maximilian Swayne seated to his left. He did a double take and sputtered, "Who …? What …?"

The apparently world-famous musician shook Joey's hand and stated, "*Who* is Maximilian Swayne, and *what* depends entirely on who you ask about me."

Joey found his voice and asked, "What are you doing here?"

Jason looked across at Mr. Swayne and said, "If you will allow me to answer that. Today we're going to be talking about money, and Mr. Swayne and Mr. Forbes have a lot to say on the subject."

Joey stared at Maximilian Swayne openmouthed until the rock star finally spoke, explaining, "Joey, Miss Sally and I were great friends for many years. Just as my career was taking off, a wise business manager gave me the gift of a few days at Anderson House. During my stay, I happened to meet Mr. Forbes and other frequenters of the bed-and-breakfast, who taught me many lessons, including how to handle money.

"Most musicians spend their lives trying not to starve to death. A few of us find lightning in a bottle and discover ourselves surrounded with everything we thought we ever wanted. At that point, most of my colleagues somehow manage to squander it all and find themselves facing starvation again.

"Thanks to the hard work and resourcefulness of your family, you were born with the lightning already in the bottle, but you've got to learn quickly how to manage your money and make it an asset for the world instead of a liability for you."

Joey seemed confused and bewildered.

Jason interjected, "If you'll allow me, I'd like to share my grandfather's thoughts on the topic."

Red Stevens appeared on the screen and spoke. "Today, we are going to talk about what may, indeed, be the most misunderstood commodity in the world. That is, money. There is absolutely nothing that can replace money in the things that money does, but regarding the rest of the things in the world, money is absolutely useless.

"For example, all the money in the world won't buy you one more day of life. That's why you're watching this videotape right now. And it's important to realize that money will not make you happy. I hasten to add that poverty will not make you happy either. I have been rich, and I have been poor—and all things being equal—rich is better.

"Jason, you have no idea or concept of the value of money. That is not your fault. That is my fault. But I am hoping in the next thirty days you can begin to understand what money means in the lives of real people in the real world. More of the violence, anxiety, divorce, and mistrust in the world is caused by misunderstanding money than any other factor. These are concepts that are foreign to you because money to you has always seemed like the air you breathe. There's always more. All you have to do is take the next breath.

"I know that you have always flashed around a lot of money and spent it frivolously. I take the responsibility for this situation, because I deprived you of the privilege of understanding the fair exchange between work and money."

The room fell silent as we all felt the weight of Red Stevens's words.

Steve Forbes broke the silence. "Joey, money's like most things in life. You can only learn so much theory, but if you're going to really master anything, you've got to have some practical lessons."

Joey seemed bewildered. Steve Forbes fixed him with a stare. "Thanks to Mr. Hamilton's invitation, Mr. Swayne here and I"—Steve Forbes put his hand on the shoulder of the rock star beside him and continued—"support a children's hospital through a foundation I run with Mr. Hamilton's help. Mr. Swayne has agreed that he and his band will play a benefit concert here at Anderson House's amphitheater next month with all the proceeds going to benefit the children we serve and their families."

Joey still appeared to be grasping for some sort of meaning in all this, so I explained, "Son, you and Jason are going to organize the event, work with all the sponsors and patrons, collect the funds, and then—in what I hope will be an experience you will never forget—you are going to determine how best to present the money to those who need it most."

Joey protested, "I've never done anything like that, and I don't even know where to start."

Mr. Forbes closed our breakfast meeting by saying, "Joey, it's like anything else. You start at the beginning, and you do one thing at a time until the goal is reached. And if I might add a piece of advice, never focus on the money."

This sounded baffling coming from the world's leading authority on finance.

He continued, "If you focus on money, your priorities will always be wrong; however, if you focus on the people you're serving, the colleagues you are working with, and the task you are performing, the money will always take care of itself."

CHAPTER EIGHT

THE LEGACY OF FRIENDS

Some friendships are a legacy left to us by those who have gone before. Other friendships are legacies we will leave behind.

Miss Hastings kept me apprised of all of the details and the progress of the upcoming benefit concert. Her reports suggested that Joey was performing well, if a bit hesitantly at first. We scheduled a breakfast meeting at Anderson House two weeks before the concert to go over all the details.

As we enjoyed all of Claudia's culinary delights, Mr. Forbes ran through the preparations that had been set in motion by his foundation for the upcoming event. Maximilian Swayne assured us that he and his band would be ready to "rock the house," as he described it, and his manager had alerted their entire fan base via social media, with which I am not entirely familiar. Jason updated us on the sponsors, media coverage, and advertising.

Finally, I turned to Joey and said, "And now, it's time for your report."

Joey cleared his throat, hesitated a moment, and then stated, "I have been to the children's hospital a number of times." He seemed to grow emotional and then said, "The kids are really amazing. A lot of them are in pain and facing life-threatening problems, but they seem to carry on as if nothing is out of the ordinary. Their families, on the other hand, are obviously worried about their kids and dealing with unbelievable financial burdens …" Joey looked down at the table, seeming to contemplate what he had experienced. "I have never seen anything quite like that. These people are really hurting, and I'm glad we're going to be able to help them with money from the concert."

After Joey concluded all the details of his report, I spoke. "On behalf of Mr. Forbes's foundation and the children's hospital, I want to thank everyone for their efforts. Not only are we helping Joey understand the lessons about money Miss Sally wanted him to learn as part of her legacy, we are doing work that would make her proud."

I directed my comments to Joey and continued, "She also wanted you to learn about friends and friendship, and since we are putting on this wonderful concert, I wondered if you might be able to get at least three of your friends to fly in for the show and to stay for a week afterward in order to help us with the presentations and arrangements we'll be undertaking to benefit the children and their families." I interjected a doubtful tone into my voice and said, "You probably don't have any real close friends like that."

Joey slapped his hand on the table and pointed his finger at my face, saying, "You have no idea about me and my friends. I have friends all around the world. They've gone with me sailing, mountain climbing, sightseeing, to sporting events, and to other things you don't know anything about. I can get a lot more than three friends here."

I smiled and nodded amicably, assuring him, "No, son, I probably don't know much about it, and we'll all look forward to meeting your friends here at Anderson House for the concert and the work we will do the following week." I assumed my lawyerly countenance and tone, stating, "But make no mistake, Joey. While we're doing good things for a great cause, this is still a part of your great-grandmother's bequest that I'm overseeing. We will expect and require you to have three friends here as a part of the lesson Miss Sally wanted you to experience."

The breakfast meeting broke up, and Joey still seemed to be angry and distant. He slipped away without giving me an opportunity to say good-bye before I left Anderson House.

The night before the benefit concert, Miss Hastings and I arrived at the stately bed-and-breakfast, settled into our customary rooms, and walked across the grounds toward the amphitheater. As we approached the concert venue, I could hear the band tuning up their instruments.

When Miss Hastings and I reached the amphitheater, we took seats in the back row and looked over the setting. The band fell silent and looked at one another as if preparing to play.

I was fearing another audio assault of the sort I had heard when Joey played their latest album but was shocked to hear the keyboard player and guitarist Maximilian Swayne combine their efforts on a melodic, stirring rendition of Pachelbel's Canon.

As the last notes faded into the distance, Miss Hastings and I walked down the aisle and greeted Maximilian Swayne and the band.

I looked at the rock star and commented, "I'm exceedingly impressed with your musical selection. I didn't realize that you and a composer that lived five centuries ago could collaborate in such a special way."

Maximilian Swayne chuckled and replied, "An old music teacher of mine told me there's no such thing as a good kind or bad kind of music. There are only good players and bad players. Pachelbel's *Canon in D* was one of Miss Sally's favorites, so the guys and I thought, since she's resting right over there on the hill, we would offer up our own sort of tribute."

I have found that the pleasant surprises in life come not from the things we know but from the things we thought we knew before we had the opportunity to relearn them.

Joey approached at that moment, pushing a young girl in a wheelchair toward the stage. She was tiny, seemed very frail, and had several casts and bandages in evidence, but she was smiling brightly, and her eyes shone with an intelligence and energy that was captivating.

Before Joey could utter a word, she proclaimed, "My name is Stephanie; I'm seven years old, and I was in an accident, but I'm getting better."

She pointed behind her and continued, "This is my friend Joey. We have been doing radio and TV interviews to help the concert."

She looked at Maximilian Swayne adoringly, and he welcomed her. "Stephanie, it's good to see you again. Let me introduce you to some of my friends."

The little girl had an amazing time as the band prepared for the concert scheduled for the following day.

The next morning at the breakfast table, Joey introduced me to a number of his friends whom he had flown in—courtesy of his dwindling trust fund—for the concert and the week of work we would be doing with the children's hospital. I may have seen a more disheveled and disreputable group of humanity sometime in my eighty years on earth, but I couldn't remember when.

The day was bright and clear, which was a relief. Weather is always a concern for an event such as a benefit concert in an outdoor amphitheater, but everything went off without a hitch.

The packed house responded enthusiastically to Maximilian Swayne and his band, though I will admit to not appreciating the music from the concert as much as I had enjoyed their rendition of Pachelbel's Canon the night before.

Mr. Forbes took the stage during intermission to thank everyone for their generous support of the children's hospital, and the crowd was appreciative and respectful, with the exception of Joey's friends, who were rude and disruptive. Several of the security guards got them to at least quiet down to a certain degree, and then the show went on.

All in all, I would say it was a near-perfect day that benefited a great cause.

As my head hit the pillow that night, I was tired but grateful for all that had happened and slept the sleep known only by those who have done good work for a great cause.

The next morning, as I settled into my place at the breakfast table, I greeted Steve Forbes and Maximilian Swayne and thanked them for all that they had done to make the event a success.

Jason and Miss Hastings were excitedly recounting episodes from the concert when Joey entered dejectedly and flopped into his chair at the far end of the table without making eye contact with anyone.

I addressed him. "Good morning, Joey. As I mentioned to you, we need three of your friends to join us for this meeting, which will involve a lesson in friendship."

He muttered something I couldn't hear, so I declared loudly and firmly, "Speak up, son. We can't read your mind."

He shot an angry look at me and shouted, "They've all gone! None of my friends would stay. They took the round-trip tickets I bought for them, rescheduled their flights, and flew home after the concert. They didn't want to do any work for the hospital."

Joey paused, and Jason slipped discreetly from the room.

Joey hung his head and admitted, "I guess they really weren't as good of friends as I thought they were, and this probably blows my inheritance, whatever that was going to be."

An officer of the court and a practitioner of the law often has to enforce things they would rather not deal with.

I sighed in resignation and explained, "Joey, the provisions of your great-grandmother's will and the instructions you received did, indeed, require you to have three friends present. I'm not left with much choice ..."

At that instant, Hawthorne opened the door and Jason pushed young Stephanie in her wheelchair into the room.

She greeted everyone cheerily. "Good morning, everybody. I heard that all of Joey's friends were getting together, and we were having blueberry pancakes."

Miss Hastings turned toward me and whispered, "That's one."

Jason chimed in. "That's right. Stephanie and I were just talking about it, and since we both like blueberry pancakes and are both friends of Joey's, here we are."

Miss Hastings whispered, with a bit of emotion in her voice, "That's two."

I resumed my legal proclamation. "Well, Joey, you have two friends here, but ..."

Hawthorne cleared his throat forcefully and interrupted. "Sir, if I may. I was honored to count Miss Sally among my friends, and she spent many hours sharing her hopes and dreams for her great-grandson, Joey, with me. I feel as if I know him and would be pleased to count him among my friends."

Joey shook his head, rejecting the notion, and spit out, "Look, I don't need your help or your pity, Hawthorne. You weren't friends with my great-grandmother. You just worked for her."

Hawthorne stood at attention, stared at Joey, and stated for all concerned, "Young man, you work for your employer. You serve your friends. I am pleased and privileged to say that I worked for Miss Sally for approximately six months. I have served here for over fifty years, to date."

The room fell silent until Jason said, "I thought before we go any further, I would share what my grandfather taught me about friends."

I was pleased to see that Jason had added some video footage—outtakes that Red had not included in Jason's original Ultimate Gift message. Every word from Red Stevens seemed like a treasure to me, because I knew there would never be any more.

Once again, Red Stevens spoke from the large screen across the room.

"*Friend* is a word that is thrown around far too easily by people who don't know the meaning of it. Today, people call everyone they know their friend. Young man, you're lucky if you live as long as I have and can count your real friends on the fingers of both hands.

"A friend is not someone who makes you happy all the time, but instead, they make you better. Friends share the greatest joys and the deepest sorrows you will face in your life, and you are privileged to share their highs and lows as well.

"Friends don't always tell you what you want to hear; they care enough about you to tell you what you need to know.

"Friendship is never an even fifty-fifty split. Both of you have to be 100 percent invested in the relationship, no matter what.

"The foundation of every friendship has to be trust and respect.

"Your friends will never be perfect, nor can they expect you to be perfect, but you all expect the others to always strive to do better. Accepting the flaws of a great friend is like an investment you make in a valuable treasure. The investment seems insignificant compared to the reward.

"The whole world is looking for someone who will treat them like a friend. Instead of looking to find a friend, seek situations where you can be a friend, and you will always find what you are looking for."

The room fell silent. Joey slowly rose from his chair and walked to the doorway where Hawthorne was standing.

Joey extended his hand and said, "Thank you for being my friend."

Miss Hastings turned toward me and, with tears streaming down her face, said for all to hear, "That's three."

CHAPTER NINE

THE LEGACY OF LEARNING

The things we learn are a legacy we receive. The things we teach are a legacy we leave behind.

As the days and weeks after the concert flew by, Joey had many hands-on experiences that reinforced the lessons Miss Sally wanted him to have as part of her legacy through Red and Jason Stevens.

Joey experienced hard work as he had never known before. While he had sweat, strained muscles, and gotten blisters from the manual labor with Gus on the memorial gardens, Joey found that following up on a million details, dealing with all manner of personalities and individuals over the phone and in person, and depending on others to meet important deadlines is stressful, hard work that takes a toll on one's mind and spirit instead of one's body.

Joey confronted experiences with money he had never imagined in his short, carefree life of leisure. Money was now not just something to be spent on a whim for nothing more than personal satisfaction. Money became the tool that could provide answers to real people's life-and-death problems.

Furthermore, Joey came face-to-face with that age-old financial reality that arises when one is trying to do good work and stop suffering: there's never enough money to go around. He had to make some hard decisions that I could tell weighed heavily on his heart and spirit.

His experiences with his new friend Stephanie involved both work and money. He was trying to find money so she could get the rehabilitation treatment she needed after her accident and to subsidize her family's diminished income and increased expenses. But there simply wasn't enough to go around.

Joey and I were seated on the veranda watching the sunrise. He was lamenting, "I wish I knew how to handle the money better. I wish I knew who I could help the most and the best. I wish I knew how to raise more money."

I agreed with him. "Joey, as life goes on, you will learn many more things that will open doors to you that will raise further questions, creating more things you wish you knew."

He started to protest the mystery and enigma that I had presented him with, but I interrupted him.

"Jason may have some of the answers for you downstairs at breakfast."

Joey and I took our places at either end of the long breakfast table. Miss Hastings and Jason were present, along with Oscar and young Miss Stephanie, whose wheelchair had been pushed up to the breakfast table. On the other side of the expansive antique table was a group of people—some whom I knew personally and others I knew only by reputation.

As Claudia served everyone, I nodded at Jason to take the lead.

He got everyone's attention and began. "Joey and everyone, I want to thank you for being here, although Claudia's cooking should prove to be thanks enough.

"As you are all aware, Joey's great-grandmother opened Anderson House many years ago, and just prior to her death, she and Mr. Hamilton drew upon an experience my grandfather, Red Stevens, had prepared for me, which became known around the world as the Ultimate Gift."

Jason introduced each of the guests, among them a PhD in physics from a renowned university, the curator of an elite museum, an internationally known astronomer, and one of the country's most famous best-selling nonfiction authors. After handshakes and pleasantries were exchanged, Jason motioned toward the large video screen and played the message Red had recorded for him that had to do with learning.

"As you know, I never had the benefit of a formal education, and I realize that you have some kind of degree from that high-toned college we sent you to that is little more than a playground for the idle rich.

"Now, before you get your feelings all hurt, I want you to realize that I respect universities as well as any type of formal education. It just wasn't a part of my life. What was a part of my life was a constant curiosity and desire to learn everything I could about the people and world around me. I wasn't able to go to school very long after I learned to read, but the ability to read, think, and observe made me a relatively well-educated man.

"But learning is a process. You can't simply sit in a classroom and someday walk offstage with a sheepskin and call yourself educated. I believe the reason a graduation ceremony is called a commencement is because the process of learning begins—or commences—at that point. The schooling that went before simply provided the tools and the framework for the real lessons to come.

"In the final analysis, Jason, life—when lived on your own terms—is the ultimate teacher. My wealth and success have robbed you of that, and this is my best effort to repair the damage."

After the video ended, Jason stood and shared with everyone the details of the month he had spent in South America as a part of Red Stevens's lessons on the gift of learning. He explained, "I met the poorest people I have ever known while I was in Ecuador. But they didn't seem to understand they were living in poverty. They treasured things like family, friends, and honor, and had a very special celebration of life. I worked in a library that didn't have the quantity or quality of books we would expect to find at a garage sale."

Jason gazed around the room, and then his face took on a faraway expression, as if he were seeing it all once again.

"The native people there had a reverence for books that I am still trying to understand and embrace. I stay in touch with them to this day and will for the rest of my life. I think those people have lived through so many revolutions and seen their government overthrown so often that turmoil and poverty have become the norm. They know that someone can take all of their possessions, but no one can ever take their joy, honor, or most importantly, the things they have learned."

The eminent and learned guests at the table then began a lively discussion about science, art, religion, and the origin and meaning of life. Even though the guests were from a variety of disciplines, their knowledge seemed to support and build upon one another's and elevate the overall dialogue.

I looked down the long table and saw that Joey's eyes had a glazed-over look generally observed among bored college students. I cleared my throat and requested everyone's attention.

"Ladies and gentlemen, I want to thank each of you for being here and in your own way contributing to Joey's legacy of learning from Miss Sally. Listening to the learned and erudite conversation, I realize we could be here all day and only create more questions and identify new areas to explore, but at this juncture, I want Joey to understand what will be expected of him in the coming days."

Joey's head lifted as if he were only now fully conscious of his surroundings and paying attention.

I continued, "Joey, during the coming days, as a part of your great-grandmother's legacy, you will be asked to learn from someone, and then, just as importantly, you will be expected to teach someone."

Joey looked at the professors and learned men and women seated at the table and asked, "Who?"

I smiled and replied, "Two among us have agreed to act as your teacher and your pupil."

I let the suspense build for a moment, anticipating the lesson in learning that was about to commence. Then I explained, "You will be asked to teach our Miss Stephanie something of your and her choosing."

Joey smiled and appeared relieved, muttering, "No problem."

Joey and Stephanie exchanged a high five.

I continued, "And you will be asked to learn something of your and his choosing under the direction of Oscar."

Joey's head swiveled toward Oscar, and his mouth dropped open in shock. I waited for his anticipated verbal assault.

"What in the world am I supposed to learn from the maintenance man of my great-grandmother's bed-and-breakfast?"

Everyone around the table smiled patiently.

Joey's confusion deepened. He turned to Oscar and blurted, "No offense. I just mean ..."

Oscar nodded and said, "No offense taken, Master Joey. I am proud to be the maintenance man at Anderson House and look forward to our sessions in the coming days."

Joey declared angrily, "I'm not going to—"

I interrupted him, stating, "Joey, before you embarrass yourself further and before we adjourn this meeting, I suggest we all take a little tour with my friend Oscar."

Everyone rose and followed Oscar out of the room, down a long corridor, through a hidden panel in an out-of-the-way hall, and down a hidden flight of stairs into a magnificent library that was housed underneath the entire south wing of Anderson House.

Joey was in shock, and most of the other guests were enjoying his discovery, as they had been in the world-class library many times.

Jason was maneuvering Stephanie's wheelchair down the last of the stairs, and she enthusiastically uttered the universal verbalization of awe for seven-year-olds. "Wow! This is cool!"

I chimed in. "Yes, Stephanie, I would most heartily agree. And now I'm going to ask Oscar to tell us what we're looking at."

Oscar spoke with a confidence and clarity he exhibited only when working on a difficult maintenance project or spending time in his library.

"This is Anderson House's private library. Miss Sally, her husband, and his parents spent over a century acquiring, restoring, and cataloging the volumes you see before you. Scholars, world leaders, artists, and seekers of knowledge from all around the world travel here as many of these volumes can be found nowhere else."

Joey spoke. "Okay, this is really amazing, but what does this have to do with me learning from a maintenance man?" He looked directly at Oscar and challenged, "How many of these books, if any, can you honestly say you have read and understood?"

Oscar gazed toward the ceiling, momentarily lost in his thoughts, and then responded, "Well, I've read them all. That's easy. But to ever say you've totally understood something is a form of ignorance. Some of these books I've read several times, and with each reading, I find both more answers and more questions."

Joey stared in wonderment as the world-renowned thought leaders and scholars disappeared among the myriad book-filled shelves, following Oscar, the maintenance man who would now be Joey's teacher.

CHAPTER TEN

THE LEGACY OF PROBLEMS

As we live our lives well, we receive a legacy of problems and leave a legacy of solutions.

The practice of the law is literal, logical, and linguistic, all at the same time. It is part science and part art.

Even though the Internet and corresponding digital age have made research faster and easier, there are still many obscure legal briefs and precedents that need to be researched the old-fashioned way. I took several opportunities throughout the ensuing weeks to utilize the extensive law library at Anderson House. During each of these research visits, I observed Oscar and Joey in deep concentration and ongoing dialogue over numerous volumes in the extensive library.

I was, therefore, not surprised that when Oscar joined Jason, Joey, Miss Hastings, and me for breakfast on the appointed morning weeks later that he gave a very favorable response regarding Joey's lessons and that which he had learned.

Oscar reported, "Joey is a quick learner with the most important characteristic any student can have—curiosity."

Oscar smiled at Joey, who just looked down at the table, seemingly embarrassed, then continued. "Instead of focusing on one area, we undertook an introductory overview of a number of subjects that are a part of any learned person's lifelong pursuits. I can honestly say that Joey has the ability to be a great learner, and more importantly, he has the passion for it."

I smiled with satisfaction and thanked Oscar for his efforts in the teaching process and his report of Joey's progress.

I was shuffling some papers to go on to the next phase of Miss Sally's renovation project on her great-grandson when Miss Hastings alerted me that Oscar wasn't done speaking.

I glanced up and inquired, "I'm sorry, Oscar. Was there something else?"

He nodded hesitantly and spoke. "Sir, I reported to you what Joey had learned from me, but I would be remiss if I didn't share what I learned from Joey."

Oscar had everyone's full attention, and I will admit to being more than a little curious about where this was heading.

"Mr. Hamilton," Oscar admitted, "I have made learning a part of my life. Not as something I do but as who I am. I have learned many things from our library here and the ongoing stream of learned and prominent guests who come to Anderson House, but in my time with Joey, I realized that my learning was theoretical, and he has experienced the literal and practical."

I couldn't imagine what Oscar was trying to convey but motioned for him to continue.

"I have read about the pyramids, studied the maps of the South Pacific, and enjoyed many accounts of expeditions, but Joey has been to the pyramids, explored the South Sea Islands, and seen the summit of Mount Everest on a clear day above the South Col."

Joey was staring at Oscar as he continued his report.

"While I hope Joey will continue exploring the world of books and take every opportunity to meet and converse with learned and accomplished people, I also hope he will allow me the benefit of hearing more about his life experiences and maybe even give me the opportunity to tag along at some point in the future."

Joey nodded affirmation and thanks to Oscar, and I proclaimed, "Joey, you and Oscar have exceeded my expectations and, I believe, those Miss Sally would have had for you in the first part of this lesson about learning. However, as you know, part of learning and a key tenet of legacy is passing value on to others. To this end, you were to instruct young Miss Stephanie and experience learning from the other side.

"Unfortunately, I understand that Stephanie has been facing some very serious health challenges, and her recovery has not been progressing as we all hoped and prayed it would; therefore, we will take up that matter later."

I nodded to Jason, who announced, "The next lesson my grandfather taught me after the gift of learning was about problems. I will admit I thought he was crazy when he started trying to teach me this, but I thought he was *insane* when he told me problems could be something good. Instead of hearing from me, let's hear from him."

Jason pushed a button, and Red Stevens joined us at our breakfast meeting once more.

"Jason, life is full of many contradictions. In fact, the longer you live, the more the reality of life will seem like one great paradox.

But if you live long enough and search hard enough, you will find a miraculous order to the confusion.

"All of the lessons I am trying to teach you as a part of the Ultimate Gift that I am leaving you through my will are generally learned as people go through their lives facing struggles and problems. Any challenge that does not defeat us ultimately strengthens us.

"One of the great errors in my life was sheltering so many people—including you—from life's problems. Out of a misguided sense of concern for your well-being, I actually took away your ability to handle life's problems by removing them from your environment.

"Unfortunately, human beings cannot live in a vacuum forever. A bird must struggle in order to emerge from the eggshell. A well-meaning person might crack open the egg, releasing the baby bird. This person might walk away feeling as though he has done the bird a wonderful service when, in fact, he has left the bird in a weakened condition and unable to deal with its environment. Instead of helping the bird, the person has, in fact, destroyed it. It is only a matter of time until something in the bird's environment attacks it, and the bird has no ability to deal with what otherwise would be a manageable problem.

"If we are not allowed to deal with small problems, we will be destroyed by slightly larger ones. When we come to understand this fact, we live our lives not avoiding problems, but welcoming them as challenges that will strengthen us so that we can be victorious in the future."

I was pondering the wise words of my dear departed friend when I looked up and noticed that someone had wheeled Miss Stephanie into the room. She was seated in her wheelchair near Joey.

I smiled and greeted her, saying, "Good morning, Miss Stephanie. I understood that your physical therapy was going to preclude you from joining us today."

She seemed confused and leaned over to Joey to whisper in his ear. He whispered back into her ear, and then she smiled, nodded, and spoke.

"Joey told me that if I don't understand a word I should ask. I now know what *preclude* means."

Miss Hastings emitted a muffled laugh. I looked at her in mock scorn, saying, "Nothing wrong with a bit of a vocabulary lesson, Miss Hastings."

I nodded toward Joey and Stephanie. They conferred briefly between them, and Stephanie reported, "Joey found out that since the accident, I have missed so much school I was going to have to repeat the second grade. But he called my teacher and got all of my lessons and classwork so he could bring everything to the hospital. We've been having school every day between my therapy sessions and the other stuff the nurses make me do."

Stephanie looked toward Joey, and he continued the report. "I'm very pleased to announce that due to Stephanie's hard work, she has caught up on all of her classwork and is actually ahead of the other students in the second grade. I was so impressed with her progress, I contacted the school counselor, and Stephanie will be tested later this year to see about getting her into a gifted program."

Miss Hastings led the spontaneous applause, and we all cheered for Stephanie and her academic achievements.

I was ready to dismiss our breakfast meeting when Joey interjected, "But that's not all that happened."

I nodded for him to continue.

"Well, it kind of goes along with the gift of problems. I was able to teach Stephanie her second-grade lessons, but the amazing thing is what she taught me."

Everyone looked toward Joey with curiosity and great anticipation as he explained, "I always thought if you were sick, you were sick; and if you were hurt, you were hurt. I assumed that whatever the doctors told you was pretty much how things were going to be … However, Stephanie has taught me about the mind/body connection."

I was fascinated and motioned to Joey to tell me more.

"Well, with some of Oscar's books and Stephanie's daily examples, I learned that doctors can give you their opinion or even an idea of what you might normally expect, but we get to decide what happens to us. So even if the doctors say you're not going to get well or be able to do certain things, maybe you can."

Stephanie nodded at Joey in a matter-of-fact way, as if she assumed everyone knew that.

I was lost in thought for a few moments and then adjourned our enlightened breakfast meeting by saying, "On behalf of Miss Sally, I want to express thanks to Oscar, Stephanie, and Joey—not only for performing well in the recent days, but for allowing us all to learn something in the process."

CHAPTER ELEVEN

THE LEGACY OF FAMILY

Family is a legacy we receive and one we pass along. Some of our family members are connected by blood—others through love.

Miss Hastings and I arrived at Anderson House early in the afternoon the day before our next session with Joey was scheduled. We enjoyed tea in the parlor with Hawthorne, Claudia, and Oscar, which gave all of them an opportunity to report on the status of their respective areas of the Anderson House operation. I was pleased to learn that the reservations and cash flow were on par with the previous year, and regular patrons seemed to want to visit the special place in the aftermath of Miss Sally's passing.

After I had concluded my tasks as executor of Miss Sally's estate, which included being responsible for oversight of Anderson House, I enjoyed sitting and talking casually with the three of them. In addition to being special friends, they were an important part of Anderson House and Miss Sally's legacy.

Hawthorne concluded our discussion over tea and cookies by saying, "The only matter left undone is how to deal with the absence of Miss Sally. She was a vital part of everything we do here."

I nodded thoughtfully and responded, "I certainly agree, but while Miss Sally can never be replaced, I am hopeful that her spirit, energy, and legacy will live on here in the future."

I thanked the three senior staff members of Anderson House for their time and thorough reports, as well as for their friendship.

Miss Hastings and I took advantage of the waning daylight to take a walk on the Anderson House grounds. Without consciously thinking about it, our walk logically concluded by taking the path to the memorial gardens that surrounded Miss Sally's grave and passing through the wrought-iron gate. Miss Hastings and I stood silently and solemnly near the grave for several moments.

She broke the silence, saying, "Mr. Hamilton, she would be very pleased with the work you and Jason have done thus far with Joey."

I sighed and admitted, "We've come a long way, but Joey has no idea how far we have to go."

The next morning, Joey joined Miss Hastings and me at the Anderson House breakfast table. A few moments later, Jason entered with his bride of less than a year, Alexia, on his arm. Jason was positively beaming with pride and joy.

Alexia had always been an attractive young lady, but in the past year, I'd noticed that she was transforming into one of those women who would be an enduring beauty throughout her life. We all greeted the couple, exchanging pleasantries.

Claudia worked her culinary magic, and Hawthorne hovered on the periphery in case anyone needed to draw upon the bottomless well of his skills and experience.

At what I hoped was the appropriate moment, I got everyone's attention and said, "Today, we are here to discuss and learn about one of the most important elements of Miss Sally May Anderson's legacy. It is the Legacy of Family.

"When my lifelong friend, Red Stevens, came to me several years ago and wanted to correct and repair some problems in his own family, he looked to his grandson, Jason, and what has become known to many who followed the odyssey in the media as the Ultimate Gift. I felt at the outset I would share the thoughts of Red Stevens on the subject. From the beginning of his business career, I acted as Red Stevens's attorney, but unlike many of my other clients, Red was always able to communicate best by speaking for himself."

I nodded to Hawthorne, who dimmed the lights slightly. Jason was looking about frantically for the remote control.

I smiled and quipped, "I've got it, son. Don't worry about it."

I took the remote control out of my pocket and pressed the button Miss Hastings had shown me earlier, and then Red Stevens appeared and began to speak.

"Now, Jason, I realize that our family is about as messed up as a family can be, and I accept my full share of responsibility for that. However, the best or worst family situation can teach us a lesson. Either we learn what we want or, unfortunately, we learn what we don't want in life from our families. Out of all the young men in the world, I have selected you. I have asked Mr. Hamilton to undertake this monumental task on my behalf for you. It's hard to understand why that means something, but I want you to know that it does.

"Families give us our roots, our heritage, and our past. They also give us the springboard to our future. Nothing in this world is stronger than the bond that can be formed by a family. That is a bond of pure love that will withstand any pressure as long as the love is kept in the forefront.

"It's important for you to realize that families come in all shapes and sizes. Some very blessed people are able to live their whole lives as part of the families they were born into. Other people, like you, Jason—through a set of circumstances—are left without family other than in name. Those people have to go out and create family."

Hawthorne brought the lights back up, and I turned to Joey and said, "Joey, your great-grandmother wanted to make sure you received the benefits of the lessons and legacy the Stevens family built."

Joey interrupted belligerently, "That's fine for them, but what does this have to do with me and my family? Their family was dysfunctional, but mine is nonexistent."

I nodded and admitted, "I understand, son, and can't disagree with what you're saying. I didn't know your parents or your grandparents very well, but I knew Miss Sally, and I understand what she's trying to do here, so I thought I'd let her tell you herself."

I nodded to Hawthorne who dimmed the lights again, and I pushed Play on the remote control once more. The image of Sally May Anderson appeared on the large flat-screen TV. She looked energetic, excited, and full of life. Little did I know that it would be the last time I would ever see her, but I was grateful I had this video, which we'd shot during her last visit to my office, and I was even more grateful that I could share it with Joey now.

Miss Sally cleared her throat, looked directly into the camera, and spoke. "First, I want to thank my friend Ted for indulging an old lady in all of this … There was never a better attorney or friend than Theodore J. Hamilton."

I reached into the breast pocket of my jacket for my linen handkerchief. My allergies tend to act up while at the Anderson House due to all the gardens and plant life. Miss Hastings put her hand on my forearm in a gesture of comfort and loyalty.

Miss Sally continued, "And there was never a better friend to my friend than Miss Hastings …"

I leaned toward Miss Hastings and whispered, "The old girl was right."

As Miss Sally continued, Miss Hastings seemed to experience the same challenge with seasonal allergies.

"I also have to thank my dearly departed friend Red Stevens for blazing the trail for me on how I would like to leave my legacy behind. If there were any trailblazers left in the twentieth and twenty-first centuries, Red Stevens was certainly one of them.

"And I also have to thank Jason Stevens, Red's grandson, for helping me make my legacy live on. I never even got to talk to

Jason about doing this, but Mr. Hamilton assured me that Jason Stevens would do the right thing. No one ever received a higher compliment."

I had never known before that moment that Jason suffered with allergies as well.

Sally went on. "I want to express my eternal gratitude to Hawthorne, Claudia, and Oscar, who have been friends, confidants, and my family for over a half a century."

I was pleased to observe that the trio was standing beyond the breakfast table, taking in Miss Sally's treasured words for them.

She continued, "Now, I want to speak to my great-grandson, Joey. I know your parents and grandparents were never really a part of your life, and to the extent they abandoned you, it was probably a good thing. I know you've already learned from Jason about Red Stevens's gift of money, so I'll just say our family never had the benefit of Red's wisdom until now.

"Your parents and grandparents saw money not as a tool to do anything, but as an excuse to do nothing. Joey, I hope in the coming days, you will come to understand and embrace all that I want you to have and become. If you will keep your mind and heart open, you will not only change yourself, you will change the world.

"And, finally, my dear Joey, I want to thank you for the gift you've been to me. Many people don't live long enough to enjoy their grandchildren, much less their great-grandchildren, as they grow into adulthood. But I have watched you grow into what I believe to be the shell of a great man, and with the help of those around you today, you can be filled with the power, wisdom, and love I want you to experience.

"I know you didn't have a good family before now, but before you feel sorry for yourself, just look around the room at the best family anyone's ever had."

Miss Sally paused to collect her thoughts, nodded primly, certain she had included everything, and concluded, "To my family there, I leave you my thanks and my love. Be well always."

The screen faded to black, and we were left with an immense silence and void.

After what could have been a few seconds or several minutes, I realized that Hawthorne had raised the lights, and everyone was looking to me. I simply motioned toward Joey and asked, "Well, son. How do you feel about it now?"

It was obvious to everyone that Joey had been touched deeply, but he still disagreed with part of the lesson, saying, "I never knew any of that until she was nearly one hundred years old, and now that I know how she felt, she's already gone … What good is that?"

I was frantically wracking my brain for something to say when Alexia spoke up.

"Mr. Hamilton, if you will permit me …"

I nodded, and she continued, "Joey, you and I have just met, but I feel as if I know you, because in many ways, you are the mirror image of my dear husband, Jason."

Jason nodded his thanks to his young bride.

She smiled mischievously and continued, "Except, Joey, you're a lot smarter and might be better looking."

We all laughed, which felt good after the emotional roller coaster we had just gone through.

Alexia continued. "I know what it's like to lose someone. My daughter, Emily, was the most amazing, special little bundle of humanity you could imagine. She brought love and joy into my life. She brought Jason and me together and changed everyone she met … She's been gone over a year now, and I miss her every hour of every day. But I've realized that the way I can keep her alive and make her legacy matter is to share the love and joy that she gave me with everyone. And, Joey, I believe you can do the same thing."

CHAPTER TWELVE

THE LEGACY OF LAUGHTER

Laughter is a gift the world sorely needs and a legacy we must pass on.

The routine around Anderson House began to settle into something closer to normal after Miss Sally's death and the memorial service on the grounds. Joey struggled with his new emerging understanding of family and how the lessons he was learning might apply to him and his future life.

Hawthorne, Claudia, and Oscar reached out to him in a hundred subtle ways, slowly drawing him into all of the activities and routines that made Anderson House what it was. Jason checked in on Joey regularly, and I got daily reports from Hawthorne that were filtered through Miss Hastings.

Joey continued to visit and spend time with Stephanie virtually every day.

Sensing that the reality of life without Miss Sally was weighing upon everyone, I was glad that Joey and the rest of us were in for a dose of laughter—at least according to the notes I'd made regarding the legacy Miss Sally wanted to leave her great-grandson.

Our next session was a bit of a departure, as it did not involve getting together for breakfast, which had become customary.

Instead, I planned a casual dinner in the dining room followed by an evening in the Anderson House theater.

Miss Hastings and I arrived in the afternoon so that we could get settled into our accommodations and ensure all was in readiness. As the dinner hour approached, we strolled into the dining room, where Jason, Joey, and young Stephanie had already gathered.

As we were greeting one another, several other dinner guests arrived. One of Jason's closest friends, David, whom he had met during his Ultimate Gift odyssey, walked in with the aid of a white cane.

Joey had noticed David approaching and seemed to be uncomfortable with the prospect of socializing with a blind person.

As was his custom, David immediately banished any formality or discomfort calling out, "Good evening, everyone. You all look splendid."

Several chuckles could be heard.

Jason welcomed his friend. "It's good to see you, David."

"I always figured it was good to see anything," David quipped.

Jason directed David toward Joey and made the introductions. "Joey, this is one of my best friends, David."

Without hesitating, David said, "Nice to meet you, Joey. Great tie, by the way."

Joey glanced down quickly and then turned red, realizing he wasn't wearing a tie. Laughter filled the room.

The last two guests to arrive wore matching tuxedos. Like me, they were at least octogenarians, but they had an energy and sense of humor that belied their age. Introductions were made all around, and everyone found their places at the dining table.

Hawthorne got everyone drinks as Claudia began serving appetizers. I proposed a toast.

"May we drink to one of Miss Sally's favorite sentiments, 'When in doubt, just laugh.'"

Glasses clinked, and a pleasant dinner conversation ensued.

After a sumptuous meal, we all made our way down the corridor to Anderson House's theater. It is a wonderful, ornate room suitable for lectures, live events, or movies.

After everyone found a seat, I asked Jason to introduce the evening's festivities.

Before Jason could utter a word, David said, "I was hoping for dancing girls."

As the laughter subsided, Jason said, "Well, you're stuck with me.

"One of the strangest gifts my grandfather prepared for me was the gift of laughter. I really had a hard time finding anything funny about all of the things he was making me do as a part of my inheritance, but as I look back on them now—as is the case with most things in life—I can find the humor if I just look for it."

Jason clicked a small remote control, and a slide appeared on a screen at the front of the theater. Several chuckles could be heard in anticipation of Jason's remarks.

"Here we see our beloved friend Gus Caldwell with his infamous cattle prod."

Jason paused as more laughter erupted.

Stephanie looked at the image on the screen and asked, "What's a cattle prod?"

Miss Hastings answered, "Honey, it's something you use to make cattle go in the right direction, but Gus used to use it to wake up Jason."

"Was Jason going in the wrong direction?" Stephanie asked.

More laughter could be heard, and one of the tuxedoed gentlemen said, through his own laughter, to the other, "This kid's funny."

The other responded, "Yeah, I know. I'm writing this stuff down."

Jason shared other slides of himself at Gus's ranch.

"Here's a picture of my first effort at building a fence."

"That's pathetic," David added. "A blind guy could build a fence better than that."

One of the tuxedoed gentlemen spoke loud enough for all to hear over the laughter. "Three million comedians out of work, and the blind guy is trying to horn in on our gig."

Jason waited for the laughter to settle and said, "Mr. Hamilton arranged for a few comedy classics before we get on with the rest of our plans for the evening."

As the theater darkened and jerky black-and-white images appeared on the screen, David slipped a small earpiece into his ear so he could hear the description provided by the Narrative Television Network. I have always been amazed that a totally blind man, with the help of a bit of narration from Susan Crane and the other award-winning narrators, could capture the drama, emotion, or—in this case—humor of what everyone else was watching.

We enjoyed my favorite Marx Brothers film, an Abbott and Costello classic, and several other great comedic routines from the early days of movies and television.

Miss Hastings spotted it first, pointing at the screen and crying, "That's them!"

It was, indeed, our two elderly guests, sixty years earlier, engaged in an outrageous comedy sketch.

In the theater, one of them said to the other, "I think you're wearing the same tuxedo."

The other responded, "No, I gave that tux away. I think you're wearing it now."

After the film ended, the two gentlemen stood, accepted the applause of the small but enthusiastic audience, turned toward one another, and bowed, bumping their heads together, as they had done a million times before for generations of adoring fans.

Jason moved to the front of the auditorium again and said, "It's good to laugh, and it's good to be here with friends, but before we go any further, I want to share with you what my grandfather told me about laughter."

Jason took his seat, and Red Stevens appeared on the theater's screen.

"This month, you are going to learn about the gift of laughter. The gift of laughter I want you to learn about is not a comedian in a nightclub or a funny joke. It is the ability to look at yourself, your problems, and life in general, and just laugh. Many people live unhappy lives because they take things too seriously. I hope you have learned in the last six months that there are things in life to be serious about and to treasure, but life without laughter is not worth living.

"This month, I want you to go out and find one example of a person who is experiencing difficulties or challenges in his or her life but who maintains the ability to laugh. If a person can laugh in the face of adversity, that individual will be happy throughout life."

As the screen faded to black, Jason stood and said, "During that month, I found someone experiencing challenges who laughed about it as much then as he does now. He makes me laugh, and I know he always will, because he'll always be my friend. Thank you, David, for honoring me by being here."

"You promised dancing girls!" David shouted.

We all laughed and felt better about ourselves and our world.

CHAPTER THIRTEEN

THE LEGACY OF DREAMS

The wonders of the modern world around us are the legacy that dreamers who have gone before bequeathed to us.

It was only a few days after we'd had our experience with the oasis of laughter in the theater at Anderson House that we gathered at the breakfast table.

I glanced around to make sure everyone was in their places and then began.

"Good morning. Today, as a part of Miss Sally's bequest for Joey, we are going to deal with one of the most significant topics my friend Red Stevens presented to Jason as a part of the Ultimate Gift.

"Dreams, and the fulfillment of them, are the exclusive territory of great people. When we learn about work, money, family, or friends, we are talking about things that everyone has in greater or lesser amounts. When we talk about dreams and becoming a dreamer, we are talking about being elevated to a place that few people ever really experience. For this reason, I am going to ask Jason to share the video his grandfather left for him so that Red can speak for himself as someone who was truly one of the greatest dreamers of all time."

Jason started the DVD.

Red spoke. "Jason, this month you're going to learn about a gift that belongs to all great men and women—the gift of dreams. Dreams are the essence of life—not as it is, but as it can be. Dreams are born in the hearts and minds of very special people, but the fruit of those dreams becomes reality and is enjoyed by the whole world.

"You may not know it, but Theodore Hamilton is known far and wide as the best lawyer in the country. I know that performing at that level was a dream of his when I met him, and he has been living that dream for over fifty years. The dream came true in his heart and mind before it came true in reality.

"I can remember wandering through the swamps of Louisiana, dreaming about becoming the greatest oil and cattle baron in Texas. That dream became such a part of me that when I achieved my goals, it was like going home to a place I had never been before.

"I have been trying to decide, as I have been formulating this ultimate gift for you, which of the gifts is the greatest. If I had to pick one, I think I would pick the gift of dreams because dreams allow us to see life as it can be, not as it is. In that way, the gift of dreams allows us to go out and get any other gift we want out of this life.

"Jason, the best way to introduce you to dreams is to acquaint you with some dreamers. I knew many throughout my life. I always considered my friendship with the dreamers to be a treasure.

"One of the first truly great dreamers I ever met in my life had a passion to create places and things that would touch the imagination of people. This passion was with him all the days of his life. He had his share of setbacks and failures as well as many detractors. I never saw him or talked to him at a time when he didn't want to share his latest project with me. He was in the habit of creating huge dream boards that he would hang on the wall and draw out the plans for each of his projects on.

"I remember that when he was on his deathbed, he had arranged to tack the plans for his newest project onto the ceiling of his hospital room. That way, he could continue to look at his dream as he constructed it in his mind.

"A reporter came to visit him while he was in the hospital, and my friend was so weak he could barely talk. So, he actually moved over and asked the reporter to lie on his bed with him so the two of them could look at the plans on the ceiling while my friend shared his dream.

"The reporter was so moved that a person would have that much passion while dealing with a serious illness in the hospital. The reporter concluded his interview, said good-bye to my friend, and left the hospital.

"My friend died later that day.

"Please do not miss the point. A person who can live his entire life with a burning passion for his dream to the extent that he shares it on his deathbed—that is a fortunate person. My friend had his dream with him all the days of his life. It continued to grow and expand. When he would reach one milestone of his dream, another greater and grander one would appear.

"In a real way, my friend taught a lot of people how to dream and imagine a better world. His name was Walt Disney.

"But let me warn you. Your dreams for your life must be yours. They cannot belong to someone else, and they must continue to grow and expand.

"I had another friend whose name you would not know. He said it was his dream to work hard and retire at age fifty. He did, indeed, work hard and achieve a degree of success in his business. He held on to that dream of retiring, but he had no passion beyond that.

"On his fiftieth birthday, a number of us gathered to celebrate both his birthday and his retirement. This should have been one of the happiest days of his life—if his dream had been properly aligned. Unfortunately, his entire adult life had been spent in his profession. That is where he had gained a lot of his pride and self-esteem. When he found himself as a relatively young man without his profession to guide him, he faced the uncertainty of retirement. It was something he thought he had always wanted, but he discovered quickly it created no life-sustaining passion for him.

"A month later, my second friend committed suicide.

"The difference between one dreamer who was still energized by his lifelong passion while on his deathbed and another dreamer whose goal was so ill-fitting for his personality that he committed suicide should be apparent to you.

"Jason, it is important that your dream belong to you. It is not a one-size-fits-all proposition. Your dream should be a custom-fit for your personality, one that grows and develops as you do. The only person who needs to be passionate about your dream is you."

I could tell that everyone was deeply touched by Red's words and challenged to pursue their own dreams.

I explained, "I was there when Red made that video, and he introduced me to Walt Disney many years ago at this very table. As familiar as his thoughts and words are to me, Red's concept of living the dream still moves me deeply. I have found over the years that when we keep our dreams to ourselves, they are sort of a mythical fantasy that we don't really take too seriously, but when we share them with others whom we respect and can trust, our dreams begin to take shape and become a part of our reality."

I took a moment to make eye contact with each person around the table and continued. "I think it would be fitting if each of us shared a dream we have for our own life and future with the group.

"Since this lesson has been a part of your life and the legacy you received, Jason, I'll ask you to go first."

Jason nodded confidently and began. "When my grandfather gave me the Ultimate Gift and all the lessons included in it, I had never thought about dreams other than thinking about more things I wanted to do or have for myself that someone should give me or provide for me. After I realized the magnitude of the Ultimate Gift, the dreams I have for my life all involve sharing the lessons I have learned with others."

Jason looked across the table to Joey, nodded, and continued. "Only when I give away the legacy my grandfather gave me can I keep his memory and his dreams alive."

I thanked Jason, turned to Miss Hastings, and nodded.

She said, "Well, sir, I have always seen my dreams in the context of performing duties that help people like you, Red Stevens, and Miss Sally make their dreams come true. I have always been proud of the fact that while I don't often dream the big dream, I make it possible for others to achieve it, and then it becomes reality for us all."

I nodded and responded, "Yes, you do, and you do it as well as anybody ever did it. Many dreams have come to life because of your diligence and persistence."

Miss Hastings blushed and responded with a bit of emotion in her voice, "Thank you, sir."

I nodded toward Oscar, who had joined us for the session. He announced, "My dreams involve learning more from all the books I keep here in the library, but I also want to learn from experiences around the world that can bring those theories to life."

Oscar and Joey nodded at each other in agreement.

Hawthorne was standing next to the doorway, and I motioned to him to speak.

He cleared his throat and began. "My dreams have always been connected to Anderson House and Miss Sally. I believe I would like to dedicate the rest of my life to making sure that future generations will be able to come here and experience all that this place has to offer."

I nodded and thanked him for sharing his dream and for his longtime service to Anderson House and Miss Sally.

I had been debating whether or not to call on young Miss Stephanie, as I didn't want to embarrass her by having her try to share concepts that might be far beyond her years, but when I asked if she wanted to say anything, she leaped in without hesitation.

"My dreams would only be two things right now. First, I would like to go to Disney World like the man was talking about." She pointed toward the blank video screen on the wall, then turned back to me and continued, "And the other thing is, I want to be able to walk again."

I was absolutely speechless, without a clue of what to say next.

Stephanie explained, "My parents say because of all the medical bills, we don't have any money to go to Disney World. And I heard the doctors tell my mom that I wouldn't be able to walk any more. So that's why I want to walk through Disney World."

We all smiled and nodded encouragingly toward Stephanie, but the tears rolling down our cheeks revealed the true emotion everyone was feeling.

Finally, I turned to Joey and encouraged him to share.

He said, "While I listened to Red Stevens talking on the video, I thought about dreams, and I realized that I didn't really have any. Then, when the others were sharing, I knew that I had never felt anything like that before. But when Stephanie shared her dreams, I realized my dream is to help her go to Disney World and be able to walk again until I can find some dreams of my own."

I nodded with satisfaction, realizing that Red Stevens had presented the concept of becoming a dreamer to us all, but young Stephanie had made it a part of each of our lives, especially Joey's.

CHAPTER FOURTEEN

THE LEGACY OF GIVING

Giving a gift is an act involving one person giving to another.
Giving a legacy can touch the whole world.

I had been out of state working on a difficult trial for several weeks. The matter was resolved the day before the next scheduled breakfast meeting with Joey and everyone at Anderson House. I had made arrangements with Miss Hastings for her to collect all of my critical correspondence and bring it with her to the bed-and-breakfast so I could catch up on the issues that had piled up at the office during my absence.

I flew most of the night, sleeping fitfully on the plane. It is questionable whether airline seats are suitable for sitting, but I would testify under oath that they are definitely not suitable for sleeping.

I arrived at Anderson House early in the morning just a few moments before the breakfast meeting was scheduled. I dropped off my luggage in my suite, picked up an envelope that had been slid under my door, rushed downstairs, and was greeted by Miss Hastings as I hurried down the hallway.

We exchanged greetings, and then she asked, "How did the verdict go in the trial?"

I possess a great ego but never want to appear boastful, so I gave Miss Hastings my standard answer for court cases in which I had been victorious: "I'm pleased to say that justice was served."

She nodded as if she had expected nothing less and smiled broadly, and then we took our places at the breakfast table.

Claudia was just topping off my coffee in a mug that appeared to be larger than normal. She explained, "Good morning, sir. I felt a stout cup of coffee today might go beyond pleasant and approach medicinal."

I just nodded and began drinking the coffee.

When the other participants of the breakfast meeting were all at their places and had received their food, I decided it was time to get started. Maybe it was because I had been battling in the courtroom every day for several weeks, or maybe it was because I hadn't received my required minimum of seven hours of sleep the night before, but I spoke with a very curt, legalistic, and almost confrontational tone.

"Joey, I know that things have been going fairly well as a result of each of the lessons we have been experiencing through your great-grandmother's directives and the invaluable contributions from Red and Jason Stevens; however, there are some things I feel we must review. Sally May Anderson's last will and testament is very clear and rigid with respect to the fact that you must complete each lesson satisfactorily, demonstrating both an academic understanding and a practical application of the principles set forth."

Joey seemed bored and just nodded dismissively.

I felt challenged by his attitude and continued. "Let us make no mistake. If you fail, in any way, with respect to one of these lessons, I will be duty bound to stop the proceedings and dispense of your great-grandmother's estate in the alternative fashion she set forth in a confidential document."

The room took on an awkward silence, and I nodded to Jason. He appeared a bit hesitant and flustered, which may have been a result of my verbose legal admonitions.

He cleared his throat and began.

"The next lesson my grandfather gave to me was the gift of giving. It is a really important part of the Ultimate Gift, because the gift was given to me, and I will be giving it away to others from now on. Here's what he had to say."

Jason started the DVD player, and Red appeared, saying, "This month, I want you to learn about the gift of giving. This is another one of those paradoxical principles like we talked about several months ago. Conventional wisdom would say that the less you give, the more you have. The converse is true. The more you give, the more you have. Abundance creates the ability to give; giving creates more abundance. I don't mean this simply in financial terms. This principle is true in every area of your life.

"It is important to be a giver and a receiver. Jason, financially, I have given you everything that you have in this world. But I violated the principle involved in the gift of giving. I gave you money and things out of a sense of obligation, not a true spirit of giving. You received those things with an attitude of entitlement and privilege instead of gratitude. Our attitudes have robbed us both of the joy involved in the gift of giving.

"It is important when you give something to someone that it be given with the right spirit, not out of a sense of obligation. I learned to give to people my whole life. I cannot imagine being deprived of the privilege of giving things and part of myself to other people.

"One of the key principles in giving, however, is that the gift must be yours to give—either something you earned or created or maybe, simply, part of yourself."

My attitude transformed during the viewing of that video. Maybe it was the words and spirit of my best and oldest friend, or maybe it was because as the video was playing I had glanced at the contents of the envelope that had been slipped under my door.

I gathered my thoughts, resolving to have a more cordial, giving tone than I had displayed earlier.

Just as I was beginning to speak, Miss Hastings interrupted, saying, "Mr. Hamilton, if you will allow me."

I didn't have a clue what she had in mind or why she was interrupting, but I had discovered over the years that Miss Hastings was generally in the right place at the right time and was prepared to do the right thing. So I nodded and sat back to listen.

She picked up a file from the table in front of her and flipped it open, announcing, "Mr. Hamilton has been traveling for the past few weeks and asked me to bring his mail to Anderson House with me so we could review it. I thought now might be a convenient time."

"Miss Hastings," I admonished, "I hardly think this is an appropriate ..."

She held up a hand and smiled, displaying a familiar twinkle in her eye, and continued. "Sir, if you will indulge me."

I sighed, nodded, and prepared to listen. When you've been a friend and colleague with someone for decades, they earn the benefit of the doubt and a bit of latitude. Miss Hastings was certainly entitled to a bit of patience on my part.

She picked up one of the letters from the file and explained, "After our last session regarding the gift of dreams, Mr. Hamilton received this letter, which I felt I should share with everyone."

As if on cue, everyone interrupted and objected in unison. I couldn't imagine what was going on, but Miss Hastings begged everyone's indulgence, asked everyone to trust her, and began reading the letter.

"'Dear Mr. Hamilton, after Joey's last session on the gift of dreams and after learning about Stephanie's medical bills and her family's financial situation, I wanted to write to you to formally request funds from the Red Stevens trust to cover all family expenses and medical bills, which may include bringing in some specialists to help in what we hope and pray will be Stephanie's full recovery.

"'Thank you for handling this and for all you have done for my grandfather, me, and everyone we serve.

"'Jason Stevens.'"

Miss Hastings set the letter back on the table, and everyone looked toward Jason. He appeared somewhat confused and slightly offended, saying, "Miss Hastings, that was a confidential letter I wrote to Mr. Hamilton as my attorney regarding legal matters involving my grandfather's trust. The entire matter was to be handled anonymously, and—"

I interrupted Jason, directing my gaze to Miss Hastings, saying, "Miss Hastings, Jason is absolutely right. Under no circumstances should you have read the contents of that ..."

Miss Hastings just smiled beatifically, signaled for silence, and continued. "Gentlemen, I would totally agree with you under normal circumstances, but you two have not been privileged to have read this next letter."

She picked up another letter from the file and began reading aloud.

"'Dear Theodore, I appreciate our long association as I am privileged to be a co-laborer with you in the service of our friend and employer, Miss Sally May Anderson.

"'As you know, I was left certain discretionary funds for the purpose of maintaining and promoting Anderson House. I am going to beg your indulgence and request the widest possible discretion as I allocate funding for Miss Stephanie's medical care and family expenses.

"'I appreciate your attention to this matter.

"'Respectfully, Hawthorne.'"

Hawthorne gazed at Miss Hastings questioningly as she picked up another letter and continued.

"'My Dear Mr. Hamilton, as you are aware, our library at Anderson House remains in a constant state of flux. New volumes are acquired while others become redundant or outdated. Recently, it has come to my attention that several of our antique medical texts—which have been the envy of numerous dealers—may have reached a point in the marketplace where they should be liquidated.

"'One of the institutions that has always expressed an interest in acquiring these particular volumes is an eminent university hospital and research facility. I have contacted them regarding Anderson House donating these particular books with the stipulation that they would cover Miss Stephanie's medical bills and give her physicians access to their cutting-edge research doctors.

"'I'm writing you to ask you to formalize this transaction in a legal document covering each of these issues.

"'Sincerely, Oscar.'"

Oscar nodded and gave Miss Hastings a knowing look as she set his letter down and picked up another.

"'Mr. Hamilton, I know that I have not been very respectful or easy to deal with, so you probably won't appreciate me asking for a favor, but Stephanie and her family need my help.

"'I am not sure what, if any, inheritance I will receive from my great-grandmother, and I have no idea when I will get it, but is there any way I can borrow it or cash it in to help with medical bills and expenses?

"'Thanks, Joey.'"

Miss Hastings turned to me with tears in her eyes and said, "Sir, I trust you might excuse my revealing the contents of your confidential correspondence."

I brushed a tear from my eye and nodded affirmatively.

Miss Hastings smiled and said, "I just felt that these letters demonstrated a complete understanding and are the absolute epitome of what Red Stevens had in mind in light of the gift of giving."

I cleared my throat and spoke.

"I want to thank each of you for your letters, and I want to thank Miss Hastings for sharing them here today. While they do demonstrate the spirit and essence of giving defined by Red Stevens and demonstrated throughout her life by Miss Sally, your letters are incomplete until I share this one."

I slipped the envelope from my pocket, unfolded the page inside, and spoke. "It reads, 'Mr. Hamilton, when we all told our dreams at breakfast, you didn't have one that you shared, so if you don't have your own, you should come to Disney World with me.'"

I wiped away a few more tears with my handkerchief, paused to compose myself, then continued.

"The correspondence is signed 'Stephanie' and features an outstanding colorful illustration of Mickey Mouse."

I held up the page for all to see. Stephanie beamed from where she sat in her wheelchair at the breakfast table.

I addressed her. "Young lady, in my office downtown, I have a number of photographs and mementoes I have collected over the years that I display on my proverbial Wall of Fame. This letter will be appropriately framed and proudly displayed on that wall between the photographs of our current governor and the President of the United States."

Stephanie clapped and squealed, proclaiming, "Wow! Way cool."

It was indeed.

CHAPTER FIFTEEN

THE LEGACY OF GRATITUDE

While we are grateful for the legacies others have left us, the only tribute we can give to those who have gone before is to leave our own legacy.

The reports over the next few weeks informed me that Jason and Joey were spending a lot of time together, both around Anderson House as well as at the children's hospital, assisting Stephanie and her parents. Apparently an old man like me and videos from my dear friend Red Stevens could only teach Joey so much, but a young man like Jason was able to relate to him in tangible ways.

Several days before our next scheduled breakfast meeting, Joey and Jason asked Claudia to pack enough food to last them for a couple of days, and they hiked across the Anderson House property toward a small spring-fed lake near the distant boundary where a tiny cabin had stood since the main house was built over 150 years before. The two young men spent the following days and nights hiking, fishing, swimming, and sitting by a fire talking late into the night. I think it took both Jason and Joey some time to realize how similar they were and how much they had in common.

Growing up poor the way I did, I don't think I could have related to the trials and tribulations faced by young people of extreme wealth. Wealth comes with privileges but also with many responsibilities and a number of burdens.

In the ensuing years, I have noticed that people with a certain amount of fame, success, or wealth have to find someone who has attained a similar station in life if they're going to relate their own problems and challenges.

Later, I learned that one evening in the cabin by the lake, Jason shared the video his grandfather had made for him about the gift of gratitude. Using his cell phone, Jason had somehow stored all of Red's video messages so they were with Jason at all times.

I remembered being an observer in the corner the day Red Stevens delivered that message in front of the camera we had set up in a conference room in our law offices. I will always remember his image on the screen and his valuable words for his grandson …

"When you prepare your will and a video like this, you automatically have to think about your entire life. I have been so many places and experienced so many things, it is hard to remember that I have only lived one lifetime.

"I remember, as a young man, being so poor that I had to do day labor for food to eat, and had to sleep along the side of the road. I also remember being in the company of kings and presidents and knowing all of the material things this life has to offer. As I look back, I am thankful for it all.

"During what, at the time, I considered to be some of my worst experiences, I gained my fondest memories.

"Jason, this month, you are going to learn a lesson that encompasses something that has been totally lacking in your life. That is gratitude.

"I have always found it ironic that the people in this world who have the most to be thankful for are often the least thankful, and somehow the people who have virtually nothing many times live lives full of gratitude.

"While still in my youth, shortly after going out on my own to conquer the world, I met an elderly gentleman who today would be described as homeless. Back then, there were a lot of people who rode the rails, traveling throughout the country doing just a little bit of work here and there in order to get by. It was during the Depression, and some of these so-called hobos or tramps were well educated and had lives full of rich experiences.

"Josh and I traveled together for almost a year. He seemed very old at that time, but since I was still in my teens, I may have had a faulty perspective. He is one of the only people I ever met of whom I could honestly say, 'He never had a bad day.' Or if he did, there was certainly no outward sign of it. Traveling about as we did, we often found ourselves wet, cold, and hungry. But Josh never had anything but the best to say to everyone we met.

"Finally, when I decided to settle down in Texas and seek my fortune there, Josh and I parted company. Settling down was simply not a priority in his life. When we parted, I asked him why he was always in such good spirits. He told me that one of the great lessons his mother had left him was the legacy of the Golden List.

"He explained to me that every morning before he got up, he would lie in bed—or wherever he had been sleeping—and visualize a golden tablet on which was written ten things in his life he was especially thankful for. He told me that his mother had done that all the days of her life and that he had never missed a day since she shared the Golden List with him.

"Well, as I stand here today, I am proud to say I haven't missed a day since Josh shared the process with me over sixty years ago. Some days, I am thankful for the most trivial things, and other days I feel a deep sense of gratitude for my life and everything surrounding me.

"Jason, today I am passing the legacy of the Golden List on to you. I know that it has survived well over one hundred years simply being passed from Josh's mother through Josh to me, and now to you. I don't know how Josh's mother discovered the process, so its origins may go back much further than I know.

"In any event, I am passing it on to you, and if you will be diligent in the beginning, before long it will simply become a natural part of your life, like breathing."

Jason and Joey arrived back at Anderson House just a few moments before our breakfast meeting was scheduled to start. Knowing that the cabin near the lake was several miles across the property over some rugged terrain, I calculated that the young men had been up long before dawn. Joey seemed to be serene but somehow very purposeful and focused in his demeanor.

Claudia served Jason and Joey first. Apparently, they were ravenous after their long hike, because by the time Claudia had finished serving the rest of us, they were ready for seconds.

I decided to wait until they had finished eating before beginning our discussion on gratitude. I learned many years ago in the courtroom that the mind can only grasp what the stomach or rear end can endure. No matter how intent someone is on learning, if they are hungry or tired of sitting, they can miss even an important message.

Finally Jason and Joey leaned back in their chairs and announced they were unable to eat another bite.

I savored my last sip of coffee and began.

"Red Stevens was a man filled with gratitude throughout his life. Most people who knew of him learned about him through media accounts and books that were based on the later portion of his business career and personal life. I don't think people were that impressed with Red's gratitude, as the argument could be made that, considering his wealth and fame, he had a lot to be grateful for. But I can assure you, as one of the few people who knew him in the early days, Red Stevens was grateful for everything he had even when the poorest among us would have agreed there wasn't much."

I gazed at everyone around the table and noticed that Jason and Joey were nodding in understanding.

Jason interjected. "Joey and I watched the gratitude video from my grandfather on my iPhone while we were at the cabin."

I smiled and replied, "Well, then, instead of listening to my ramblings, I would enjoy hearing what you have to say about it."

Jason deferred to Joey with a nod.

Joey reached into his pocket, took out a piece of paper, unfolded it, and set it on the table in front of him. He glanced at it for a few moments and then spoke.

"I had always thought of gratitude as saying 'Thank you' when someone gave you something. I realize now that it was just one of those phrases I uttered without thought.

"After Jason shared the video that Mr. Stevens had made, I couldn't sleep, so I walked around the lake and thought about it for a long time. I couldn't imagine that I could write down ten things I was thankful for, so I decided to try it just to prove to you it didn't work."

Everyone chuckled, and I smiled at Joey, reassuring him that I was not upset.

He looked down at the paper and continued. "Well, actually, before it was done, I realized I had more than ten things and had to leave a few off."

"Wow," Jason exclaimed. "That happens to me all the time. My golden list changes every day, with some of the items moving up or down the list or off of it completely until they reappear at some point in the future."

Joey took a deep breath and said, "Well, here goes. First, I am thankful for my new friend, Jason, since he seems to already have gone through some of the weird stuff I am dealing with now."

Joey looked up as everyone chuckled. Miss Hastings nodded encouragingly for him to go on.

"Secondly, I am thankful that I got to know my great-grandmother, if only after she died. I wish I had known her before, but at least I have her legacy."

I interjected, "Son, I knew your great-grandmother very well, and all I have left is the legacy she gave me."

Joey nodded thoughtfully, looked at his paper, and said, "Number three, I'm thankful to Oscar for the lessons he gave me and the books he loans to me.

"Fourth, I'm thankful to Claudia for the great food."

Jason smiled, looked at Claudia, who was peeking in from the kitchen door, and said, "I'll second that."

"Fifth," Joey continued, "I'm thankful to Hawthorne for everything he does at Anderson House and for being my friend.

"Sixth, I'm grateful to Mr. Forbes and Maximilian Swayne for helping with the children's hospital.

"Seventh, I am thankful for Miss Hastings for always being nice to me and making me feel like I'm going to be okay.

"Eighth, I guess I'm thankful to Gus Caldwell."

We all laughed.

Joey continued, "He taught me how to work, and I'm thankful for the gardens we built, but it took a while before I felt gratitude for hard work.

"Ninth." Joey looked directly at me and said, "I'm thankful for you, Mr. Hamilton, for being a good friend to my great-grandmother and for connecting the two of us through her legacy."

I nodded respectfully toward Joey, acknowledging his kind words. His voice grew emotional as he continued.

"And tenth, I'm thankful for all of the people who are helping Stephanie and her family. Even though the prognosis is not good, everyone has been amazing, and I am very grateful."

I replied, "Red Stevens always said, 'A man with experience never has to take a backseat to a man with a theory.' Joey, you have now experienced the gift of gratitude and the Golden List. I remember the first time I sat down and made a list similar to the one you just read to us. I thought it was an interesting challenge that Red had thrown out to me, but I couldn't imagine that I would be making a golden list every morning for the rest of my life."

I reached into my jacket pocket, took out my own sheet of folded paper, and held it up for everyone to see. I announced, "And Joey, since you were kind enough to include me in your first list, I want to share with you and everyone here that you were on my list today."

Joey seemed surprised and pleased all at the same time.

Miss Hastings said mischievously, "Mr. Hamilton, would you like to read your list aloud in case any of the rest of us made your golden list today?"

I shook my head and said, "No, I believe I'll keep it to myself, but you seem to have a permanent place on my golden list every day."

What had started out as a joke obviously touched Miss Hastings deeply after my response, and for that, I was very grateful.

CHAPTER SIXTEEN

THE LEGACY OF A DAY

Our lives are lived a day at a time, and our legacy is made up of these days.

At my age, one becomes decidedly aware of the fact that there are more days behind you than ahead of you. On one level, this can be disturbing, but on another level, it can create a sense of urgency and priority that makes each day count. I find myself far more engaged with things that matter in my life and far less patient with things that don't matter.

Miss Hastings and I had arrived back at Anderson House the afternoon before our next breakfast session with Joey. We had time to visit Miss Sally's grave and enjoy the memorial gardens that surround the burial site.

I knew Miss Sally would be pleased with the way the gardens were growing, developing, and maturing. I hoped she would be likewise pleased with Joey's progress.

I slept soundly, anticipating a special day ahead.

The following morning found me, once again, enjoying the sunrise on the veranda overlooking Anderson House's extensive grounds. I sipped my coffee and wondered how many mornings I had sat in this same place contemplating the coming day. Whether it was the seasons of the year, prevailing weather, or simply my own mood, this same view seemed to be unique and different on every occasion.

Downstairs, I was just taking my seat at the breakfast table when Joey entered, pushing young Miss Stephanie's wheelchair.

I greeted her. "Good morning, Stephanie, and how are you this fine day?"

The reports from the doctors had not been encouraging with respect to her physical therapy and rehabilitation. The thought of this vibrant young person spending the rest of her life in that wheelchair was sobering, but Stephanie seemed not to realize or simply overlooked the inevitable, saying, "Good morning, sir. I'm doing just fine. It's a great day."

As I looked at the frail seven-year-old who was bearing burdens more suited for someone much older and much more mature, I realized I had to agree with her. It was, indeed, a great day.

Miss Hastings entered with Jason. They had obviously been sharing a joke or something humorous between them. The two of them had always enjoyed a special relationship. Miss Hastings had believed in Jason when almost no one else—including me—had, and Jason seemed to be encouraged and uplifted by Miss Hastings when no one else could reach him.

Hawthorne and Oscar joined us at the breakfast table. Claudia served a sumptuous breakfast and then took a place at the table herself after everyone had been served.

I was looking forward to hearing from my best friend once again. He was never far from my heart and mind, but being a part of Jason's sharing of Red's messages with Joey made me feel like my friend was with me once again.

I greeted everyone and announced we would be discussing the gift of a day that Red Stevens had presented to Jason.

I explained, "I never met anyone who could get more out of a day than Miss Sally. I remember her telling me that if you live every day of your life as if it were your last, someday you would be right, and you would have an amazing experience all of the other days. This has impacted me greatly throughout my life, as I know it will throughout yours."

I paused to let those powerful words sink in and noticed everyone around the table nodding in agreement and paying rapt attention.

I continued, "As we look back over our lives, we realize that great things come to us on pivotal days. These are days when we meet a new person, find a new opportunity, or simply decide to change our lives by changing our minds.

"Now, I want you to hear from one of the best experts I ever met on how to live a day."

I nodded to Jason, and he pushed the button on the remote control, bringing Red Stevens's image and words into the room.

"Jason, I want you to know that as I was contemplating the ultimate gift I wanted to present to you through my will, I spent a lot of time thinking about you. I think you've gained a permanent place in my Golden List each morning. I am thankful that you and I share a family heritage, and I sense a spark in you that I have always felt in myself. We are somehow kindred spirits beyond just our family ties.

"As I have been going through the process of creating my will and thinking about my life and my death, I have considered all of the elements in my life that have made it special. I have reviewed many memories, and I carry them with me like a treasure.

"When you face your own mortality, you contemplate how much of life you have lived versus how much you have left. It is like the sand slipping through an hourglass. I know that at some point I will live the last day of my life. I have been thinking about how I would want to live that day or what I would do if I had just one day left to live. I have come to realize that if I can get that picture in my mind of maximizing one day, I will have mastered the essence of living because life is nothing more than a series of days. If we can learn how to live one day to its fullest, our lives will be rich and meaningful."

As the video faded to black, Jason spoke.

"After Mr. Hamilton shared that video with me for the first time, my assignment was to determine what I would do if I knew it were the last day of my life. That exercise caused me to think about all the ways I used to waste time and just how many precious things someone can pack into a day if they are determined to do so. As time goes by, I continue to think about that lesson, but my priorities change and grow, so the concept of how I would spend my last day here on earth constantly improves."

I thought about Jason's ideas surrounding the gift of a day and how the elements of that day might improve. As an idea formed in my mind, I shared it with everyone at the table.

"I realize that each of our ultimate days would contain many activities, but I thought it would be powerful if we would each share just one thing that would be a part of our special day."

I nodded to Miss Hastings, who, without hesitating, said, "My special day would involve helping others do what they do best. Through the years, I have worked with Mr. Hamilton, assisting many successful and talented clients, but I realized a long time ago that every one of those high-impact people has quality support people alongside them who make it possible for them to do what they do. So my last day on earth, and every day between now and then, should include helping people be their best and do their best."

I nodded to Miss Hastings and reached out to place my hand on her arm in a gesture that I hoped would convey the gratitude and respect I hold for her.

I nodded toward Jason, and he shared, "My gift of a day would have to include giving away the lessons that my grandfather gave to me through the Ultimate Gift. Because of his generosity, I control an immense trust fund through which I can help organizations and people with basic needs, but I know that unless I can help them understand the priorities in life, contained in the lessons of the Ultimate Gift, all the money in the world won't make a lasting difference."

"Jason," I intoned, "your grandfather would be proud of you, and I know that I am."

I looked toward Hawthorne inquiringly and asked, "Would you like to share?"

He nodded without hesitation and said, "My best day would involve and does involve helping the guests of Anderson House experience and discover the things they need in their lives to become who they were meant to be. When I do my job well, people have a chance to discover new things and live in better ways."

I admired the fact that a person whom many people would see as a simple butler or chauffeur could understand the impact his career and his life could have on others.

I nodded to Oscar, and he spoke.

"While it seems like my job is to maintain this wonderful place, which I am privileged to do, all of my best days include learning something I had never known before and teaching people how to learn things for themselves, both now and in the future."

I thanked Oscar and motioned to Claudia, who said, "My life and my days are meaningful when I serve others and express my love and respect to them through the food I prepare and the way I serve it. Many tremendous people have sat at this very table sharing impactful thoughts and ideas because it was a special occasion. They felt it was a special occasion because I made it special for them."

I was filled with hope as I turned to Joey and asked, "Son, what thoughts do you have on how you would spend a special day or the last day of your life?"

Joey sighed, hesitated for a moment, then admitted, "I haven't learned all of the lessons or had all the experiences that the rest of you have had. I realize from your descriptions of how you would spend your ultimate day that I have wasted many days pursuing my own wants and desires. It seems like the more days I spent doing that, the less satisfaction I got from it, so my days were often empty and even boring."

Joey hesitated. I wasn't sure if he was done speaking, but I waited a moment and was pleased when he continued.

"I've spent so many of my days recently working with Stephanie, her family, and the doctors on all of the things that are needed for her treatment. I guess if I was going to spend a special day like the rest of you are talking about, I would probably do something that Stephanie and her family wanted to do."

Joey looked at me questioningly as if he were unsure whether his answer was acceptable.

I smiled broadly and proclaimed, "I couldn't have said it better myself."

I wasn't sure whether I should give Stephanie a chance to speak. I didn't want to intimidate her in front of a group of adults, but on the other hand, I didn't want to leave her out.

I will spend the rest of my life being thankful that, on a whim, I turned to Stephanie and asked her to share what she would do on a special day.

Without hesitating and with her youthful innocence, she announced, "I would go to Disney World with my family and all of you. We would do fun things all day, and I would get to meet Mickey Mouse."

A few rare times in my life, I have spoken without thinking or considering the consequences. Before I was even aware of it, I heard myself saying, "You know, Stephanie, that's ironic, because my law firm has just established a fund for the sole and singular purpose of providing trips to Disney World for young people like you, along with their families and friends."

Stephanie cheered and applauded. Everyone else got caught up in the moment and joined in her celebration.

I thanked everyone for a special morning and exchanged handshakes and hugs as everyone left the room.

When Miss Hastings and I were alone, she turned to me with mock surprise, saying, "Mr. Hamilton, I wasn't aware of this special Disney World fund we had put in place."

Without emotion, I responded, "It's a new thing that I have just recently established."

She pointed out, "Sir, I haven't even gotten the paperwork on it."

I laughed and said, "Well, it looks like you're going to be getting a lot of Disney World paperwork very shortly."

CHAPTER SEVENTEEN

THE LEGACY OF LOVE

Regardless of the legacy we receive, love is the legacy we should leave behind.

The next few days and weeks were filled with planning, preparation, and anticipation of the trip to Disney World.

Miss Hastings was, once again, the miracle worker I had come to expect throughout our years together. Schedules were set, reservations were made, and everything was put into motion as the trip approached.

I had spoken with Stephanie's family and her doctors about their concerns with respect to the stress and exertion of the travel on her delicate condition. We finally got a cautious and somewhat guarded approval from the children's hospital to take Stephanie on the eagerly anticipated Disney World excursion. One of her doctors shared with me confidentially that he was doubtful whether her therapy and rehabilitation would result in any further improvement.

My greatest worry was about the long trip to Disney World. There would be several layovers involved, and Miss Hastings was having difficulty getting everyone booked on the same flights as it was only a few days before we were to leave.

I was sitting at my desk, contemplating the disaster that a late flight or missed connection could cause, when Miss

Hastings buzzed me to let me know that Gus Caldwell was on the phone.

I picked up the receiver and greeted him, and then I heard that familiar booming voice say, "Ted, Gus here. I've got a problem that I'm hoping you can help me with."

I slid a blank legal pad and pen in front of me, preparing to take notes on whatever details made up Gus's legal problem.

He explained, "As you know, I just bought this newfangled, overpriced jet to make my life more convenient, and now the pilots are bothering me with some noise about how the engines don't have enough hours on them, and we need to use the plane more. So I thought you could help me out.

"I heard about this little Disney World trip, and you know, Ted, I've lived more than eighty years and have never been to Disney World, so whenever Miss Hastings tells me the time is right, I'm gonna have the pilots fire up that contraption, head up there to pick you all up, and then we'll all be off to Disney World."

I stammered and stuttered, trying to find a way to express my thanks to Gus, but he interrupted. "Ted, I don't need any excuses, feedback, or legalese. As long as we've been friends, and as much as I've paid you to be my lawyer, the least you can do is help me get my pilots calmed down over this jet thing."

Without any further discussion, he said a quick good-bye and hung up.

I just sat there thinking about how many people were impacted by a simple act of love.

We were all gathered at the private airport awaiting the arrival of Gus and his jet.

Jason, Alexia, and Joey were huddled with Stephanie and her family, excitedly reviewing Disney World travel brochures and everything they wanted to do during the trip.

Miss Hastings and I were conferring with Hawthorne, Oscar, and Claudia to confirm that all of the details of the ongoing operation of the Anderson House during their absence would be handled.

Then, as if on cue, a beautiful silver bird dropped from the clouds and smoothly glided in for a landing. The jet taxied over to where we were waiting, and as the engines wound down, Gus opened the door and stood at the top of the stairs to greet everyone.

"Welcome to Disney World Express. All aboard!" he called.

That night, we had a special dinner at the house Miss Hastings had reserved for us on the Disney World property. Everyone had their own room or suite, but there was a community area where we could all gather for meals or recreation.

Just as if we were at Anderson House, Claudia took control of all of the preparations and prepared a magnificent dinner. Hawthorne and Oscar took care of each minute detail to ensure everything would be perfect.

As I approached the dinner table, Stephanie's mother whispered to me that Stephanie wanted to say grace before we ate.

After all of us were settled in our places, I thanked each person around the table for all that they had done to make this trip possible, then I nodded to Stephanie. She asked everyone to bow their heads.

She prayed, "Dear God, I want to thank You for loving us and helping us to love each other. And I want to thank You for making this part of my dream come true. Amen."

A few tears were wiped away as we settled in to enjoy a magnificent dinner.

After Claudia's dessert had been consumed and everyone assured her they couldn't eat another bite, Jason asked for everyone's attention and said, "I thought this would be an appropriate time to share the last lesson my grandfather gave me."

Hawthorne lowered the lights, and Jason pushed the remote control for the DVD player and the large screen on the side wall of the community area.

I eagerly watched my friend appear before our eyes to share his final lesson.

"Jason, in this last month, I'm going to introduce you to the one part of my ultimate gift that encompasses all of the other gifts as well as everything good you will ever do, have, or know in your life. That is the gift of love.

"Anything good, honorable, and desirable in life is based on love. Anything bad or evil is simply life without the love involved. Love is a misused and overused term in our society. It is applied to any number of frivolous things and pursuits, but the love I am talking about in the gift of love is the goodness that comes only from God. Not everyone believes or acknowledges that. And that's okay. I still know that real love comes from Him—whether or not we know it.

"Jason, we've come a long way in this ultimate gift. I want you to know, above all, that in spite of all the mistakes I made and the many times I failed you, that Jason Stevens, your grandfather loved you."

The room fell silent, and Jason spoke through the tears that had formed in his eyes. "I want to thank you all for sharing that very special lesson with me, and I want to express my love to each of you for making my life all that it is."

We enjoyed the fireworks that Disney World presents each night over the lake, and we shared thoughts, dreams, and gratitude about the love that surrounded this whole enterprise far into the night.

Eventually, everyone drifted off to their accommodations to enjoy a good night's rest.

The next morning, we gathered around the table for breakfast. I was eagerly anticipating the surprise that Miss Hastings had arranged for Stephanie. I hoped that it would be a special memory she would hold on to for the rest of her life. Little did I know it would be so much more than that for all of us.

Claudia prepared and served a culinary masterpiece, as she did every day at Anderson House. I wasn't sure how she had made arrangements to re-create the special dishes she prepared in her own kitchen when she was hundreds of miles from home.

As everyone finished breakfast and I enjoyed my second or possibly third cup of coffee, Miss Hastings gave me a clandestine signal.

I tapped my spoon against my water glass to get everyone's attention and proclaimed, "Many years ago, my friend Red Stevens and Sally May Anderson introduced me to Walt Disney. One need look no further than this incredible place to understand what kind of magical person he truly was. That fertile mind created many special characters that have become an indelible part of our lives. One of them is here this morning and asked if he could meet Stephanie."

Stephanie's eyes grew wide, and she glanced around the room eagerly.

I offered a formal introduction. "Friends, loved ones, and especially Miss Stephanie, please welcome Mickey Mouse."

The world's most famous rodent bounded into the room, greeting everyone around the table amidst laughter, cheers, and applause. He stopped in front of Stephanie and bowed.

Without thinking, and before anyone else realized what was happening, Stephanie rose from her wheelchair, took two halting steps, and fell into the welcoming arms of Mickey Mouse for a long-awaited and never-to-be-forgotten hug.

I remembered her brief prayer the night before, expressing her thanks for the first part of her dream coming true, and I remembered the remainder of her dream, which had seemed unimaginable and unattainable, was simply to walk again.

I silently offered my own thanks to heaven for making the remainder of her dream come true.

As tears of joy streamed down everyone's face, I was left with the inescapable conclusion that dreams are more powerful than a diagnosis, and love conquers all.

CHAPTER EIGHTEEN

THE ULTIMATE LEGACY

Who we are is a tribute to those who have left us a legacy.
Who we help others become will be our legacy.

I was seated in the familiar chair behind my desk in the corner office of the ornate law building of Hamilton, Hamilton & Hamilton. I gazed across the room at my Wall of Fame, which held mementos that represented treasured memories from throughout my personal and professional life. There had been some new additions to the Wall of Fame recently, including Miss Stephanie's portrait of Mickey Mouse on my invitation to accompany her to Disney World. This framed masterpiece was surrounded by a montage of photos that included Jason and Alexia standing arm in arm in front of the entrance to the Magic Kingdom; Hawthorne, a bit overdressed for an amusement park, standing beside Goofy; Oscar disembarking from his fourth ride into Space Mountain; Claudia sampling the baked goods and pastries prepared by Disney's finest chefs; Miss Hastings and me on a leisurely boat ride on the lake; Gus, dressed up in his standard western garb, with one of the many tourists who assumed he was one of the attractions; and—in what has become my favorite photo on the entire Wall of Fame—Stephanie standing with both her family and Joey beside the one and only Mickey Mouse.

Stephanie still spent a significant amount of each day in her wheelchair, but day by day and step by step, she grew stronger. The doctors were astounded, and we all knew it was only a matter of time until she would be running, jumping, and playing like every seven-year-old in the world should.

Everyone was still enjoying the afterglow of the Disney World trip as we gathered for what would be our final formal breakfast meeting dealing with the lessons of legacy that had been left to Joey by his great-grandmother.

We all stood as the last breakfast guest walked into the room. It was Stephanie wearing her Mickey Mouse T-shirt and ears. I marveled at her attitude and the rapid recovery she had experienced since the Disney World trip.

Joey helped Stephanie with her chair, and everyone took their seats.

Breakfast was served by Claudia and enjoyed by everyone. I began the session by welcoming everyone to what would be the final official meeting regarding Joey's legacy, which Miss Sally had planned for him.

I thanked Jason and, of course, his grandfather Red Stevens for making this odyssey possible. I thanked Hawthorne, Oscar, and Claudia for everything they had done throughout the proceedings, and I expressed my gratitude to Miss Hastings for her efforts on this project and everything she makes possible in my world.

Finally, I turned to Joey and stated for the record, "Joey, over the past months, throughout each of these lessons, I know there have been struggles and frustrations amidst the joy and triumph. I want to congratulate you for persevering to the end.

"Your great-grandmother did, indeed, prepare an amazing inheritance and wonderful legacy for you. The ordeal you have gone through was to ensure you were ready, willing, and able to receive the legacy, understand its value, and make it grow as a part of your own legacy.

"I believe I'll let Miss Sally express it in her own words."

I nodded to Hawthorne, who lowered the lights, and then Jason pushed Play on the remote control.

Miss Sally appeared on the video screen, seated at the conference table in my office. She appeared hopeful, if a bit tentative, as she began.

"Joey and my friends and loved ones gathered there, I want to thank and congratulate each of you on a successful journey. If you're watching this video, which I hope and pray you are, it means that my life's work and intentions for my legacy have not been in vain.

"Joey, in the coming days, Mr. Hamilton and his staff will be taking care of all the legal details involved with transferring the control of Anderson House to you. This will include everything on the property itself, as well as some significant reserve funds held in trust for the maintenance and further development of the property, along with special projects of your own in the future.

"By this time, I hope you have come to understand that Anderson House is more than just a bed-and-breakfast where people come. It is, instead, a place of healing, hope, and destiny. Throughout your life, it will continue to be a destination where people can come in order to become great, and great people can come to become greater.

"As you take over the leadership of Anderson House, you will deal with some of the most famous, successful, and prominent people of your generation. You will, also, deal with many common people who just want to make a difference in their own world. You will need to find the balance that will allow you to treat great people as if they were common, and common people as if they were great.

"You will need to always grow and learn, as Anderson House will be a reflection of your energy and spirit.

"I know my staff as well as or better than they know themselves, so I can virtually assure you that Hawthorne, Oscar, and Claudia, along with the rest of the staff, will be at your side every step of the way. You, no doubt, have also become aware of the fact that Mr. Hamilton and Miss Hastings are tremendous friends and allies that you can call on at any time.

"And, finally, I hope that you and Jason have somehow found the basis for a friendship, as you are, in a way, kindred spirits. The most daunting journey is made easier simply by traveling with another or drawing strength from those who have traveled before you.

"And if you ever need to talk with an old lady who loves you and cares about you, I'll be waiting at the top of the hill.

"I leave you all with my thanks, my best wishes, and my love."

I was so caught up in the moment that I was not ready for Miss Sally's image to fade away. It had almost felt like she was in the room with us.

I turned to Joey, whose expression was etched with the emotion we all felt. I congratulated him again and confirmed Miss Sally's assertion that he need only call on me anytime I could be of service to him or the work at Anderson House.

Before we adjourned for the last time, I offered Joey the chance to speak.

He rose to his feet and declared, "I want to thank each of you for helping me understand and become worthy of accepting my legacy. I also want to apologize to each of you for the disrespect I demonstrated throughout these months. I simply didn't know what I didn't know. I guess the root of all strife, disagreement, and evil is simple ignorance. There are times we just don't know what we are doing to others around us."

Joey reached for a box that was on the floor beside his chair and continued.

"As a small token of my thanks and on behalf of Anderson House and my great-grandmother, I would like you each to have a gift that I prepared for you."

Joey had prepared identical plaques for everyone who had been on the Disney World trip. It showed the entrance to the park and had a poem etched across the image. It read:

Hold on to your dreams and stand tall,

Even when those around you
would force you to crawl.

Hold on to your dreams as a race you must run,

Even when reality whispers you'll never be done.

Hold on to your dreams and wait
for the magic to come,

Because on that magical day,

Your dreams and your reality
will merge into one.

We all thanked Joey for the special gift, which we would each treasure for the rest of our lives.

Everyone exchanged hugs and well-wishes, and as Joey was saying his final good-byes, I inquired, "Son, I'm not familiar with the poet you immortalized here on my plaque."

I held the plaque in front of me.

Joey laughed heartily and declared, "That was actually written by a distant relative of Miss Sally's."

I was baffled, as I had never known that there was a poet in the Anderson family. I asked, "Who might that be?"

Joey stopped in the doorway and turned briefly, saying, "Oh, it was written by Sally May Anderson's great-grandson. He's discovering all kinds of new things about himself."

As evening began to envelop the Anderson House grounds, I found myself beside Miss Sally's grave. I felt a brief visit might provide closure to all that had gone before. I said what was on my mind and in my heart: "Well, old girl, I did my best. I know you would expect nothing more and accept nothing less. You can rest well, knowing that Anderson House is in good hands, and your legacy lives on."